D0992201

Mrs Pargeter's Package

One will do a lot in the cause of friendship, and it is in that cause that Mrs Pargeter finds herself setting off on a package tour to Corfu. Not her usual style of holiday, but she understands only too well the grief and need for companionship of her recently widowed friend, Joyce Dover. The journey to Corfu is uncomfortable, the company of her fellow holidaymakers less than inspiring, and Mrs Pargeter is worried by her friend's unusual behaviour. First there was that strange business in the Gatwick departure lounge, when Joyce insisted that Mrs Pargeter carry a mysterious package through Customs for her. The way its contents moved left no doubt that the package contained a bottle, but why should Joyce be taking alcohol into a country where it was so readily available . . . ?

When they finally reach their holiday destination, the beautiful little port of Agios Nikitas, Mrs Pargeter decides that she will put her troubles on one side and settle down to have a good time. Joyce, on the other hand, with too much help from a bottle of ouzo, just digs herself deeper into her trough of gloom. Her behaviour in the taverna that first evening is irrational and irritating, and Mrs Pargeter is quite relieved when it is finally time for bed.

She awakes next morning to brilliant sunshine, and the full beauty of the island is revealed. But when she goes to wake her friend, Mrs Pargeter is confronted by an horrific sight: Joyce's lifeless body lies crumpled on the bed, its wrist slashed by the jagged edge of a broken ouzo bottle. It looks like suicide, but, as Mrs Pargeter reconstructs the events that led up to her friend's death, she becomes increasingly convinced that someone else was involved. Mrs Pargeter is determined to stay on Corfu until she catches the killer.

by the same author

A SHOCK TO THE SYSTEM
DEAD ROMANTIC
A NICE CLASS OF CORPSE
MRS, PRESUMED DEAD

Charles Paris novels

CAST, IN ORDER OF DISAPPEARANCE
SO MUCH BLOOD
STAR TRAP
AN AMATEUR CORPSE
A COMEDIAN DIES
THE DEAD SIDE OF THE MIKE
SITUATION TRAGEDY
MURDER UNPROMPTED
MURDER IN THE TITLE
NOT DEAD, ONLY RESTING
DEAD GIVEAWAY
WHAT BLOODY MAN IS THAT?
A SERIES OF MURDERS

Mrs Pargeter's Package

Simon Brett

First published in Great Britain 1990 by
MACMILLAN LONDON LIMITED
4 Little Essex Street London WC2R 3LF
and Basingstoke

Associated companies in Auckland, Delhi, Dublin, Gaborone, Hamburg, Harare, Hong Kong, Johannesburg, Kuala Lumpur, Lagos, Manzini, Melbourne, Mexico City, Nairobi, New York, Singapore and Tokyo

ISBN 0-333-54273-8

A CIP catalogue record for this book is available from the British Library

Typeset by Matrix, 21 Russell Street, London WC2

Printed in Great Britain by Billings and Sons Ltd, Worcester

To Nigel, Sue, Charles and
Olivia 'I Want My Armbands' Bennett

1

As the coach zigzagged through the darkness in a grinding of gears, Mrs Pargeter reflected that this was not her preferred style of travel. She knew that she had been spoiled by the late Mr Pargeter, but felt strongly that his insistence on first class facilities at all times had been more than mere pampering. Travel, it had always been his view, was a tedious necessity, the important part of any journey was what one did on reaching one's destination, and therefore the less strain the actual business of transportation involved, the better. The cost of attaining such comfort, however high, was money well spent. It had been particularly important in the late Mr Pargeter's line of work that he always arrived anywhere with all his wits about him.

However, one will suffer a lot in the cause of friendship, and it was a mission of friendship that had brought Mrs Pargeter to Corfu in these atypical circumstances. Joyce Dover, now tense beside her, peering anxiously through the coach window at the occasional light on the hillside, had been in a bad state when she first suggested the mutual holiday. Mrs Pargeter could not but sympathise; the void left in her own life by the death of the late Mr Pargeter was still a daily ache of melancholy; and Joyce had recently lost her husband, Chris. Though Mrs Pargeter had never met the man in question, she knew what her friend was going through, she knew how much nerve proposing the trip must have required, and had been happy to agree to the proposal.

She had offered to make the arrangements herself. As well as taking the burden of such details off her friend's troubled shoulders, this would also have ensured a level of resort and accommodation in keeping with her own – admittedly rather high – standards. Money never appeared to have been a problem for Joyce, but if there had been any difficulty, Mrs Pargeter would have been happy to subsidise her.

Joyce, however, had been adamantly opposed to this offer of help. Activity, she insisted, was the therapy currently required, and arranging a holiday would be an ideal distraction for her. She and her husband had never been to Greece, it was therefore an area without prompts to painful memories, so it was to Greece that they would go.

And before Mrs Pargeter had had time to drop a few hints about the parts of Greece she thought most suitable and the hotels she thought most comfortable, the bookings were made. A fortnight's package tour in early June to Agios Nikitas on the north-east coast of Corfu. Self-catering in the Villa Eleni.

Self-catering? It was remarkable, Mrs Pargeter reflected, what one would do in the cause of friendship.

So it was in the cause of friendship that she had turned up at Gatwick Airport two hours early to check in for their charter flight. It was in the cause of friendship that she had sat at Gatwick Airport for the five hours that that flight had been delayed. Friendship had made her pretend enthusiasm for plastic food in a cramped Boeing 727 full of screaming children, and friendship now found her shaken about in the back of the coach that wheezed along the switchback coastal road from Corfu Airport to Agios Nikitas.

But Mrs Pargeter did not repine or complain. Hers

was a philosophical nature. Life with the late Mr Pargeter had taught her not to set too much store by anticipation. Don't waste energy in fear of the future, he had always said. Wait and see what happens, and when it does happen you'll be surprised at the resources you find within yourself to cope with the situation.

So Mrs Pargeter smoothed down the bright cotton print of her dress over plump thighs, let the warm air from the coach window play through her white hair, and waited to see what the next fortnight would bring.

2

'Could I have your attention, please?' The tour rep, who had identified herself in a fulsome English girls' public-school accent at Corfu Airport as 'Ginnie', shouted above the groaning of the coach's engine.

It took a moment to get the attention of all the party. After the discomforts of their journey, and in spite of the lurches of the coach, a good few had dozed off. Keith and Linda, the young couple from South Woodham Ferrers in Essex, who had just got their eighteen-month-old Craig off to sleep, complained of the interruption. Mrs Pargeter, who had provided Craig with an unwilling target for airline-food-throwing practice during the three-and-a-half-hour flight, also regretted his return to consciousness.

'Sorry,' said Ginnie, in a voice that didn't sound at all sorry. Presumably she too was feeling strained after five hours waiting for them at Corfu Airport. 'I just wanted to say that we are very nearly there. In a couple of minutes, we turn off the main road down to Agios Nikitas. I should warn you, the track down to the village is pretty bumpy.'

'What, bumpier than this one? Must have more bumps than the mother-in-law's car,' said the retired man in the beige safari suit, who at Gatwick check-in had appointed himself the life and soul of the party. Mrs Pargeter had decided at the time that a little of him would probably go a long way; the total lack of reaction to his latest witticism suggested that ten hours in his company had brought everyone else round to the same opinion. Even his weedy wife, in matching beige safari suit, was unable to raise the wateriest of smiles.

'Anyway,' Ginnie continued, 'because we're rather later in arriving than we expected . . .' – grumbles of the you-can-say-that-again variety greeted this – 'and you may be hungry . . .' – this was endorsed with varying degrees of enthusiasm – 'when we get to the village, some of you may want to go and have something to eat, and others want to go straight to your accommodation. So what we'll do is stop first at Spiro's taverna and offload those who want to eat, while the coach'll take the rest to their villas.'

'And what'll happen to the luggage of the taverna party?' asked Mrs Safari Suit.

'It'll be delivered to the villas. Be quite safe there till you've finished eating.'

'That's a relief,' said Mr Safari Suit, and then slyly added, 'Cor! Phew!' The pun had elicited only minimal response when he'd first used it in the Gatwick departure lounge. Now, on its eleventh airing, it got no reaction at all.

'Er, excuse me, Ginnie,' asked Linda from South Woodham Ferrers, 'you mention Spiro's, but there is more than one taverna in the village, isn't there?'

'Oh yes, there's Spiro's and there's The Three Brothers and there's Costa's and the Hotel Nausica. Try them all by all means, but, er, the general consensus of clients who have been here over the years is that the atmosphere at Spiro's is the best. And the food, actually.'

'Do they all have Greek dancing?' asked the Secretary with Short Bleached Hair.

'Yes, there's Greek dancing most nights, and then each taverna has a party night every week. Special menu, dancing displays and so on. Costa's has his on Friday, the hotel on Saturday, Spiro on Monday and The Three Brothers on Wednesday.'

'Oh, right, we'll try Costa's tomorrow,' said the Secretary with Short Bleached Hair to her friend.

'And are there any nightclubs?' asked her friend, the Secretary with Long Bleached Hair.

'Not nightclubs as such. Not in Agios Nikitas – though of course things go on pretty late in the tavernas. If you want proper nightclubs, you have to go along the coast to Ipsos or Dassia.'

'Oh, right, we'll try that Saturday,' said the Secretary with Long Bleached Hair to the Secretary with Short Bleached Hair.

Having fielded this flurry of questions, Ginnie turned to the coach driver and said something in fluent Greek. He laughed, though whether at the expense of his passengers or not was hard to tell.

'God, I hope we get there soon,' muttered Joyce, as the coach lurched off the main road on to a pitted, stony track. 'I'm desperate for a pee.'

'Won't be long now,' said Mrs Pargeter, in her comforting, slightly Cockney voice.

'And for a drink,' said Joyce. Her small face was tight with anxiety beneath its spray of blonded hair.

The desperation for a drink sounded greater than that for a pee. Mrs Pargeter had a moment of worry. She knew that anything offering temporary oblivion was seductive in the first bleak shock of widowhood, but her friend did seem to be giving in too readily to the temptations of alcohol. Joyce had kept going with gin and tonics through the long wait at Gatwick and taken everything she had been offered on the plane.

And then there had been that strange business with the package . . . Before they went through to the departure lounge, Joyce had suddenly asked Mrs Pargeter if she had room in her flightbag to carry something for her. 'Not that it's too heavy or anything, Melita, just don't want to be over the limit if I'm stopped by Customs.'

The package that had been handed over, and that still resided in the flightbag under Mrs Pargeter's seat, had been stoutly wrapped in cardboard and brown paper, but the way its contents shifted left no doubt that it contained a bottle. The need to take her own supplies into a country where alcohol was as readily available as Greece suggested that maybe Joyce did have a bit of a 'drinking problem'.

But her caution about the Customs had not been misplaced. The grimly-moustached officer at Corfu Airport had singled out the fifty-five-year-old Joyce, along with a couple of more obvious student targets, and insisted on her opening suitcases and flightbag. Despite a detailed search, he found nothing that he shouldn't and the suspect was allowed to go on her way.

It did seem strange, though . . . And now Mrs Pargeter thought about the incident, she realised that the Customs officer had not found any other bottles in her friend's luggage. So why had the package been given to her? What had Joyce meant about the danger of being 'over the limit'? That was even stranger.

Mrs Pargeter was interrupted by Ginnie's voice before she had time to ask Joyce for an explanation. 'Right, everyone, as we turn the corner here, we'll be able to see over to Albania. Nobody quite knows what goes on in there, so a word of advice . . . if any of you are renting out boats during your stay, don't go too close to their side, OK?'

The passengers turned to look out over the void of sea to the distant lights. A large brightly-illuminated vessel moved slowly up the centre of the channel. The atmosphere in the coach changed. Now they were so close to their destination, excitement rekindled for the first time since that distant half-hour at Gatwick before they had heard about the flight delay.

'And down the bottom of the hill there you can see the village.'

They rounded the last corner. Light spilled from the seafront tavernas and villas on to the glassy arc of a little bay. Reflected bulbs winked back from the water to the strings of real bulbs above them. At their moorings bobbed motorboats, four carbon-copy yachts from a flotilla, and sturdy fishing boats with large lamps on the bows to attract their night-time catch. Some of the older fishing vessels had eyes painted either side of their prows, luck-bringers designed to outstare the Evil Eye, a phenomenon which still had its believers on Corfu.

The road ran between the buildings and the sea. Wooden piers thrust out into the water opposite the taverna entrances. At one a stout blue caique was moored.

The coach scrunched to a halt outside a large rectangular stone building over the front of which a striped canvas awning was stretched. Beneath this, tanned holidaymakers in T-shirts and shorts sat over drinks and food, paying no more than desultory attention to the new arrivals. The sound of recorded bouzouki music, together with a smell of burning charcoal and herbs, wafted in through the coach's windows.

'At last,' said Ginnie. 'Welcome to Agios Nikitas.'

3

'I really am desperate now. Must find the Ladies. You get a table, won't you, Melita?'

'Yes,' Mrs Pargeter called after Joyce's retreating back, before picking up her flightbag and moving at a more sedate pace out of the coach. She saw Joyce hurry into the stone building, only to re-emerge a few seconds later, redirected round the side where a painted notice with an arrow read 'Toilets'. It seemed that language wasn't going to be a problem in Agios Nikitas.

This impression was endorsed by the greeting of the tall man who rose from a roadside table to greet the coach party. 'Welcome to Spiro's,' he said expansively. 'Here we will give you good time. Good drink and food to relax you after your journey. Ask Spiro what you want – anything – no problem.'

He was olive-skinned, in his fifties, but well-preserved, with muscular shoulders. Despite his bonhomie, a latent melancholy lurked in eyes that gleamed like black cherries under bushy eyebrows. The hair on his head was dusted with grey, but it still grew black in the 'V' of chest exposed by his open white shirt. He wore waiter's uniform black trousers and shoes, but carried an air of undisputed authority. He snapped fingers at the younger waiters to have the newcomers distributed to tables and drinks orders taken. From the doorway to the taverna he orchestrated the distribution of this first round, and within moments everyone had been served with glasses and bottles sweating from the fridge.

The orders had varied. Half-litres of lager, bottles of Greek white wine, Cokes, a fizzy orange for Craig from South Woodham Ferrers, a few traditionalists' gin and tonics, a couple of more daring ouzos. Mrs Pargeter, safely ensconced at a table for two with her flightbag stowed beneath the seat, did not know where Joyce had reached in her alcoholic cycle, but was in no doubt about what she herself wanted to drink. The Pargeters had developed an enthusiastic appetite for retsina on Crete, where they had spent three months after one of the late Mr Pargeter's more spectacular business coups. An all too rare sustained period of conjugal togetherness, Mrs Pargeter recollected fondly.

By the time Joyce returned from the Ladies, the coach had departed with Ginnie aboard to supervise the disposition of luggage and tired tourists, and Spiro had disappeared inside the building to supervise food orders. Joyce looked flushed and anxious, and had certainly been gone a long time. Mrs Pargeter hoped that her friend wasn't ill. There was something disturbingly jumpy in her manner, but maybe it was no more than continuing reaction to her bereavement.

'Loos are spotless,' Joyce announced as she sat down.

'Oh, good. You all right, love?'

The concern was waved aside. 'Yes, yes. Have you ordered me a drink?'

'Wasn't sure what you wanted. Try some of this?' Mrs Pargeter proffered the retsina bottle.

Joyce sniffed the contents and grimaced. 'No, thank you.' She looked round and was immediately rewarded by the approach of a young waiter, carrying paper cloths and a metal holder for oil, vinegar, salt, pepper and toothpicks. 'Could you get me a drink, please?'

'Yes, please.' Deftly he lifted the retsina bottle and glasses, slipped the paper cloth under them on to the polythene-covered table top and snapped its corners secure under elastic cords. 'What you like, please?'

'An ouzo.'

'An ouzo, of course, please. No problem.'

'Thank you. Can I ask what your name is?'

'Name, please? I am Yianni, please.'

He flashed an even-toothed smile and whisked away, his improbably slim hips gliding easily between the tables.

'Hm, how do you get one like that?' Joyce asked wistfully.

'I hadn't thought of you as on the look-out for a toyboy,' said Mrs Pargeter.

'Chance'd be a fine thing. No, first time in my life that I'd be free to have a toyboy, and now I'm fiftysomething and stringy, so nobody's going to be interested.'

'Oh, well . . .' Mrs Pargeter shrugged philosophically. 'That's the way things go. I once heard someone say that experience is the comb life gives you after you've lost your hair.'

'Sickening, isn't it? Trouble is, Melita, when you actually do have the freedom, you don't realise it. I mean, when I was about twenty I could have been having a whale of a time, lots of affairs, no strings, but did I? No, I just spent all my time worrying because nobody appeared to want to marry me. Didn't you find that?'

'Well, not exactly.' Mrs Pargeter didn't really want to elaborate. In fact, she had had a vibrantly exciting sex-life before she met the late Mr Pargeter – and indeed a vibrantly exciting sex-life throughout their marriage – but she had always believed that sex was a subject of exclusive interest to the participants.

Joyce was fortunately prevented from asking for elaboration by the arrival of Yianni with her ouzo. She diluted it from the accompanying glass of water, watched with satisfaction as the transparent liquid clouded to milky whiteness and took a long swallow, before continuing her monologue. 'Conchita's just the same as I was. I mean, there my daughter is, lovely girl, early twenties, successful career, could have any man she wants, and what does she do? She keeps falling for bastards – married men, usually – and keeps getting her heart broken when they won't leave their wives and set up home with her. Why goes that happen?'

'In my experience,' said Mrs Pargeter judiciously, 'women who always go after unsuitable men do so because deep down they don't really want to commit themselves.'

'Huh,' said Joyce. 'Well, I just wish Conchita'd settle down and get married.'

'Why? Do you really think marriage is the perfect solution?'

'I don't know. I just think life is generally a pretty dreadful business and maybe it's easier if there are two of you trying to cope with it.'

This seemed to Mrs Pargeter an unnecessarily pessimistic world-view. She had never regarded life as an imposition, rather as an unrivalled cellarful of opportunity to be relished to the last drop. Probably it was just bereavement that had made her friend so negative.

'I don't know, though,' Joyce went on, digging herself deeper into her trough of gloom. 'How much do you ever know about other people? I mean, you think you're close, you live with someone, sleep with them for twenty-five years, then they die and you realise you never knew them at all. I don't think you ever really know anything about another person.'

This made Mrs Pargeter think. It did not make her question her own marriage – she had never doubted that she and the late Mr Pargeter had known each other through and through – but it did make her ask herself how much she knew about Joyce Dover.

The answer quickly came back – not a great deal. Mrs Pargeter had met Joyce some fifteen years before in Chigwell, during one of those periods when the late Mr Pargeter had had to be away from home for a while. Joyce's husband, Chris, it transpired, was also away at the time (though on very different business), and she and their daughter Conchita, then a tiny black-eyed six-year-old, were living in a rented house till his return. The two women had seen a lot of each other for three months, and kept in touch intermittently since.

Though there was a ten-year age difference between them, they had got on from the start, without ever knowing a great deal about each other's backgrounds. Joyce, Mrs Pargeter was told, had always lived in London. Her husband Chris had been born in Uruguay, but, politically disaffected with the governing regime, had fled to England in his late teens. He had made a success of some kind of export business (dealing chiefly with Africa) and had, from all accounts, turned himself into the perfect English gentleman. His origins were betrayed only in details like his daughter's unusual Christian name. That was all Mrs Pargeter had ever known about the life and business of Chris Dover.

And she had seen to it that his wife Joyce knew even less about the life and business of the late Mr Pargeter.

Joyce maundered on, but Mrs Pargeter only half-listened. The retsina was as welcome as ever, and in the soft, warm breeze that flowed off the sea, lulled by the recorded strumming of bouzoukis, she started to relax. It had been a tiring day, and the prospect of a lethargic fortnight in the sun became very appealing. There was always, Mrs Pargeter found, something seductive about being in a new place. So many exciting details to find out when you start from total ignorance. Yes, she was going to enjoy herself in Agios Nikitas. Very relaxing, she thought, to be in a place where I know no one, and no one knows me.

Which was why she was so surprised to hear a voice saying, 'Ah, good evening. Mrs Pargeter, isn't it . . . ?'

4

The man she looked up to see was a creature of contradictions. The voice that addressed her had been thick Cockney, but its owner looked typically Greek. Heavy Mediterranean features seemed at odds with the thinness of his body, and this incongruity was accentuated by the flapping tourist uniform of brightly-coloured shorts and T-shirt. Sticklike legs ended in sports socks and improbable silver-grey trainers. He looked like a Greek trying to pass himself off as an English holidaymaker.

Responding to the blankness in her eyes, the man immediately identified himself. 'Larry Lambeth. I used to work with your late husband.'

That explained everything. The late Mr Pargeter's business interests had been wide and had involved acquaintanceship with people from a variety of backgrounds. Since he was a great believer in the separation of his domestic and professional lives, there were many of his contacts whom Mrs Pargeter had never met and she had become accustomed – particularly since her husband's death – to encounters of this kind with people she had never seen before.

'Do join us, please, Mr Lambeth. Can I get you a drink?'

'Allow me.' He called across to a waiter in fluent Greek, then sat down.

After introducing Joyce, Mrs Pargeter asked the question that was uppermost in her mind. 'I'm delighted to meet you, but how on earth did you know I was going to be here?'

'Oh, there aren't many secrets in a place like this. Everyone knows everyone, all related, you know. No, I'm sure I would have found out pretty quickly, anyway, but in fact I was tipped off.'

'Tipped off?'

'Well, that is to say I was informed by a friend back in England that you was planning a trip over here.'

'Oh?'

'Truffler Mason.'

'Ah.' No further explanation was required. Truffler Mason was one of the inestimably useful contacts featured in an address book which the late Mr Pargeter had bequeathed to his wife. The skills which had earned Truffler his nickname were now being directed into the legitimate work of the Mason de Vere Detective Agency, and he had proved invaluable to Mrs Pargeter in a murder investigation the previous year. Larry Lambeth could not have provided better credentials.

The waiter brought fresh drinks. Mrs Pargeter was still only half-way down her initial half-litre bottle of retsina, and placed the full one beside it. Joyce, who had drained her first ouzo, fell on the second with disturbing enthusiasm. Larry Lambeth had ordered a glass of Greek brandy. This would have been against the advice of the late Mr Pargeter, who, having sampled it when they were on Crete, had expressed the opinion that, though Greek brandy might well be an excellent rust-removing agent, it had no place in the human digestive system. Larry Lambeth, however, sipped at his drink with apparent fervour, before continuing his explanation.

'No, fact is, Truffler rang me last week, Mrs P. Tipped me off, like, said you was on your way, asked me to look after you, you know, see if there was anything you needed, generally help you out. And of course I said yes. I mean, it would have been a pleasure to help, anyway. I'd have done it without asking, but Mr P. – your husband, that is – he specifically asked me to keep an eye out for you, you know, if there ever was a time I could be of any assistance.'

Mrs Pargeter smiled fondly. It was always heartwarming

to find out the careful provisions the late Mr Pargeter had made for her before his death. Not every widow had the benefit of such assiduous long-term protection.

'He was the best,' Larry Lambeth asserted. 'The very best, a real prince.'

'Yes,' Mrs Pargeter agreed, a trifle mistily.

The coach drew up once again outside the taverna, having distributed luggage to the various villas of Agios Nikitas. Ginnie, a clipboard and a mess of papers clutched to her bosom, leapt lithely off the vehicle, calling out some pleasantry in Greek. The driver laughed at this parting shot, and drove off in a scream of metal. Mrs Pargeter decided that the previous noisy gear changes had not been dictated solely by the corkscrew roads; they were just part of his driving style.

At the sight of Ginnie, Mr Safari Suit, seated over pork chops with Mrs Safari Suit, called something out, but she resolutely pretended not to hear and strode towards the interior of the taverna. In her haste, she did not notice a couple of papers dislodge themselves from the bundle in her arms and float to the ground.

Mrs Pargeter picked them up, stopping Larry Lambeth who made to rise. 'Don't worry, I'll give them to her,' she said and followed the rep into the stone building.

The atmosphere inside the taverna was markedly different to that outside. It was dark and, in an indefinable way, primitive. This impression did not derive from the facilities. The gleaming aluminium refrigerated counter, through whose glass front slabs of meat, fish and lobsters could be seen; the CD-player with its attendant racks of boxed CDs; these, and the spotlessness of the marble floor, attested to the taverna's recent creation or refurbishment. In corners of the mirrored bar were tucked overflashed snapshots of giggling tourists dancing with Spiro and his waiters.

It was the faces inside that gave the primitive feeling. Through a hatch to the kitchen a black-eyed woman looked up at the newcomer's entrance with an expression of studied vacancy.

The men whose small table by the bar Ginnie had joined also turned their eyes on Mrs Pargeter. There were three sitting there with glasses of ouzo in front of them – Spiro, another, balding man with blue eyes but unmistakably Greek features, and a third dressed in uniform.

Mrs Pargeter's first impression was that he was the Customs officer who had stopped Joyce at Corfu Airport. The likeness was striking, but a closer look showed differences. The uniform was not the same, either; this man was dressed in light grey. His moustache formed a perfect black isosceles triangle over his mouth, and an upturned peaked cap lay on the table by his glass.

The ancient, slightly deterrent, curiosity in the men's eyes was echoed in the expression of a photograph over the bar. Though their owner looked old and ill, the dark eyes in the faded picture seemed to dominate the scene like some household god. The photograph's central position and lavish frame gave the impression of some kind of shrine, and the family likeness left no doubt that its subject was Spiro's father.

Mrs Pargeter was only allowed to feel like an intruder for a millisecond before Spiro's customary smile reappeared. He rose to his feet and spread his arms expansively. 'Can I help you?'

Mrs Pargeter proffered the dropped papers, which had turned out to be car-hire agreement counterfoils. 'You dropped these, Ginnie.'

'Oh, thank you so much.'

She must still have been looking at the photograph, because Spiro confirmed her conjecture. 'My father. It was taken just before he died – thirty years ago – but still he keeps an eye on his taverna. Spiro brings good luck to Spiro. The photograph keeps away the Evil Eye.'

The two other men chuckled, as if this had been rather a good joke. Mrs Pargeter gave a little grin and said, 'Oh, isn't that nice?'

The whole episode had taken less than a minute, and she couldn't explain the feeling it had given her. She had felt a *frisson*, not exactly of fear, but of sudden awareness of new complexities, of the difference between the tourist surface and reality of Corfu.

At the door she looked back into the room, hoping to recapture and perhaps further define the impression. But all she saw was joviality, the flash of friendly teeth from the men. Only in the proud defiance of the photograph, and the guarded eyes of the woman in the kitchen, could she still feel the depths to the brink of which she had stumbled.

5

When she got back to the table, their food had arrived. Joyce was toying with a lamb kebab on rice and in front of Mrs Pargeter's place was a crisply grilled fish with garnish of a few chips. Between them on the table was a bowl of Greek salad, topped with feta cheese. Joyce was working her way through yet another ouzo.

Mrs Pargeter attacked her fish with relish, while Larry Lambeth further defined his relationship with her late husband.

'Fact is, I worked with him a great deal. I mean, I was never one of the big boys, but I done kind of little jobs for him.'

'Ah.'

A look of modest pride came across his face. 'I was involved in, er . . . Welwyn Garden City.'

Mrs Pargeter looked suitably impressed. 'And now you're living out here, are you?'

'Yeah, well, I always said I'd come back to Greece. I am Greek, you see. My parents was Greek, but I was brought up in London. Lambeth, actually. Where I got the name from.'

'Really?'

'Well, growing up in London, like I did, you had to make a decision. You know, when you go into business, do you play on the ethnic bit or do you just gloss it over? I had to ask myself – do I want to spend the rest of my life known as Nick the Greek? And I decided I didn't, so I made up Larry Lambeth. Reckoned it was less conspicuous, and the sort of work I do, you don't want to draw attention to yourself too much.'

'Ah, no, I see.'

'So, you know, at home I was Greek, spoke Greek with the parents and all, but professionally I was, well, just London. So long as I done my work all right, nobody was that interested in where I come from.'

'Right. And now you've retired, have you?'

'Yeah, well, in a manner of speaking. Fact is, I always did fancy coming out to Greece at some stage . . . you know, roots and that. And, not to put too fine a point on it, there was a moment when staying in London suddenly didn't seem too brilliant an idea.' He leant towards her confidentially. 'Fact is, Mrs Pargeter, I got mixed up with a rather dubious bunch. This was after your husband died, of course. I mean, Mr P. was always a great organiser, you run no risks working for him – well, no risks other than the ones naturally associated with our line of work – but after he'd gone, I got mixed up with a real bunch of villains. And, fact is, the moment come when either I had to get out of London sharpish or I might not be able to get out of anywhere for a few years . . . if you catch my drift?'

Mrs Pargeter nodded. She caught his drift all right.

'I had my savings, and I still had my Greek passport, and I thought, well, maybe this is the moment to change all that London fog for a bit of the old Greek sunshine. So, like, end of story – here I am.'

'And you've given up work completely now, have you?'

'Well . . .' Larry Lambeth smiled modestly. 'I do run a small business on my own account . . . very small, like, but I kind of keep my hand in.' In response to Mrs Pargeter's quizzical eyebrow, he continued, 'Probably better if I don't go into too much detail, eh?'

She gave him a nod of complicity, as she negotiated a fishbone out of her teeth.

'Anyway, as I say, anything I can do for you while you're out here, no problem. That's a catchphrase out here, actually – "no problem". Got it on all the T-shirts and that. Mind you, with the Corfiots, sometimes there is problems. With me, none – promise you that, Mrs Pargeter. Anything you need, you just say the word – OK?'

'Thank you very much.'

'I mean, like, if you want to use the telephone, I got a telephone up my villa.'

'Oh? Aren't there that many telephones around?'

'No. I think Spiro's got the only telephone in Agios Nikitas. Could be one at the hotel, but, anyway, you might not want to use either of those.'

'Why not?'

'Could be a bit public. Things get overheard in a place like this. You want to make any kind of private call, you do better using mine.'

'Oh, well, thank you very much.'

'No problem. And the same goes for you, Mrs Dover, if you . . .'

He tailed off as he saw Joyce's expression. Mrs Pargeter looked at her friend, whose face was white with shock, and followed her eyeline to the opening of the taverna.

Spiro stood in the doorway with his back to them, but over his shoulder could be seen the man in uniform. His face was now squared off by the peaked cap and his expression was stern.

Joyce Dover was staring fixedly at him, mouthing soundlessly. She looked as if she had seen a ghost.

6

It was over within seconds. No one except Mrs Pargeter and Larry Lambeth noticed anything amiss. Mr Safari Suit was busily ordering Mrs Safari Suit to look more relaxed for a holiday snap. Linda from South Woodham Ferrers was trying to get Craig off to sleep again, while Keith from South Woodham Ferrers, who kept saying how great it felt to be away from the office, was punching at his calculator, working out how the price of Greek white wine compared with the Lutomer Riesling from Sainsbury's that they liked so much. The Secretary with Short Bleached Hair and the Secretary with Long Bleached Hair leant close over their lager glasses, planning their fortnight's campaign of sexual conquest.

The man in uniform was also unaware of the effect he had had. By the time he had been clapped on the shoulder and waved on his way by Spiro, Joyce had rushed from the table to the edge of the sea, where she leant over the water shaking convulsively.

Mrs Pargeter was quickly by her side. Joyce had emptied her stomach, but still shuddered with dry retching.

'There, there, love,' said Mrs Pargeter, putting an arm round her friend's shoulders. 'You all right?'

Tears, induced either by nausea or emotion, coursed down Joyce's cheeks, negating the vigour with which she nodded. 'Yes. Yes, I'm fine.'

'Did you see something that frightened you?'

'What?' A wariness came into her eyes. 'No, no, I didn't see anything. Must be something I ate on the plane. Airline food's always pretty dodgy.'

'I had the same, and I feel all right,' said Mrs Pargeter evenly.

'Something I was allergic to, perhaps.' Seeing the discreet scepticism that greeted this, Joyce tried another tack. 'I'm sorry, since Chris died, I've just been in such a nervy state, it doesn't take much to set me off. You know, you think you're in control and then suddenly you're reminded of something or you see something, and the pain of loss is right back with you.'

'Yes, I know, Joyce love.' The soothing voice hardened a little. 'And what were you reminded of just now?'

'I'm sorry?'

'Did you see something just now that set you off?'

'What? No, no, I was just using that as an example. I just had a thought about Chris and . . . you know, the fact that I was on holiday without him and . . . the emotion just got the better of me.'

'Yes, of course. I see,' said Mrs Pargeter, as if the explanation satisfied her.

'Erm, is there anything I can do to help?' Larry Lambeth, who had been hovering at a discreet distance, stepped forward to the couple at the sea's edge.

'No, thank you, Mrs Pargeter replied. 'Joyce is just not feeling very well. I think we'd better find our villa and get her to bed. Don't you think that'd be a good idea, Joyce?'

‘Yes, yes, thank you, Melita.’ Joyce Dover pulled a handkerchief out of her pocket, wiped her face and blew her nose noisily.

She turned back with some trepidation to face the taverna, and seemed relieved that the policeman had disappeared. Resolutely she walked back to their table.

‘I’ll just go and see Ginnie, find out exactly where the villa is,’ said Mrs Pargeter.

Again the atmosphere inside the taverna seemed to come from another culture, but this time without the same sense of threat. Maybe it was the police uniform which had struck the previous sinister note.

Ginnie was in conversation with the balding man. Though Mrs Pargeter couldn’t understand a word, the tone of his voice suggested that he was tearing the rep off a strip. She kept trying to remonstrate, but never got much further than the name ‘Georgio’. The man became aware of Mrs Pargeter and stopped speaking, gesturing her presence to Ginnie with his eyebrows. He went back to his ouzo as the girl turned round. She looked flushed and upset. Older, too. The rep was well into her thirties.

‘I’m sorry to bother you, Ginnie, but my friend Mrs Dover isn’t feeling very well. I think we’d better make our way to the villa now, if you don’t mind.’

‘Of course.’ Ginnie stood up. ‘I hope it’s nothing serious.’

‘Oh no, just a bit of gastric trouble. Sure she’ll be fine in the morning.’

‘Yes. The villa’s only a couple of hundred yards away. I’ll walk you up there.’

‘Thank you. I’d better just settle up for the meal . . .’

‘Spiro!’ Ginnie shouted, the name prefacing a torrent of Greek. Georgio added his own incomprehensible views of the subject.

Spiro appeared from the kitchen, his broad smile already in place. He flashed something in Greek, which sounded almost like an order, to Ginnie, then turned his beam on Mrs Pargeter. 'What can I do for you?'

'I'd just like the bill, please. My friend's not feeling too well, so I think I'd better get her into bed.'

'Yes. I hope she soon be better in the morning. It is a very healthy island, Corfu. The air is good, soon make her . . . right as rain.' He pronounced the idiom with considerable pride.

'I'm sure it will. So, if you could just tell me what I owe you . . . ?'

His hands dismissed the idea. 'No, please, I can't work it out now. Too much trouble. You pay me next time you come to Spiro's.'

'Oh, well, if you're sure . . . ?'

'Of course. No problem.'

What a nice gesture of trust. Then came the little cynical thought that of course it wasn't just a gesture of trust; it was also a way of ensuring that nice honest English people would return to eat at the taverna again.

'Can we go now? I feel dreadful.'

It was Joyce who had spoken. She leaned weakly against the doorway.

'Yes, love. We're sorted now and—'

Mrs Pargeter stopped. Once again Joyce had gone into her trance of horror. She was gazing over towards the bar counter. Behind it, the silent dark-haired woman now stood, mixing Nescafé into coffee cups. She did not register Joyce's presence, but moved across the room to hand the cups to Yianni, who swirled past to deliver them to customers outside. Then the woman retreated into the kitchen. Spiro, who did not appear to have noticed anything odd, followed her.

Joyce still gazed fixedly ahead, her face a white mask of terror.

'Come on, love,' said Mrs Pargeter, taking her friend's

arm and marching her firmly out of the taverna. 'You need to get to bed.'

Larry Lambeth still lurked protectively by their table. 'Anything I can do, Mrs Pargeter?'

'No, really. We'll be fine now.'

'Look, here's my address and phone number.' He thrust a piece of paper into her hand. 'There's an Ansaphone there, so don't hesitate to get in touch, you know, if there's the smallest thing you need . . .'

'Thank you, Mr Lambeth.'

'Please call me Larry.'

'Very well, Larry. Thank you.' Mrs Pargeter had a sudden thought and moved closer to him. 'There is something perhaps you can tell me.'

'Yes?' Larry Lambeth dropped his voice to a matching whisper.

'The man in uniform who was here earlier . . . ?'

'Mm?'

'Do you know who he is?'

'Sergeant Karaskakis. From the Tourist Police.'

'Ah. And perhaps you can also tell me—'

'Right, are we set?' Ginnie bustled towards them. 'The villa's only a couple of minutes away and—' It was the sight of Larry that stopped her in mid-sentence. She looked at him with undisguised distaste.

'Well, er, better be on my way now,' he said awkwardly, and scuttled off into the warm night.

'That man wasn't troubling you, was he?' asked Ginnie.

'No. No, actually, he was being very helpful,' Mrs Pargeter replied.

'Oh. Well, keep an eye on him. Apparently he has some kind of criminal record back in England.'

'Really?' said Mrs Pargeter, her eyes wide with naive amazement.

'Yes, and you know what they say . . . once a thief, always a thief.'

'Oh. Well, I wouldn't know about that,' said Mrs Pargeter righteously.

7

The walk from Spiro's to the Villa Eleni was magical. From the flat seashore strip, along which the tavernas and few shops of Agios Nikitas clustered, the hills rose steeply and out of their olive-, cypress- and brush-clad slopes the square, white outlines of buildings rose. By night only the villas' soft lights could be seen, pale orange-tinted rectangles in the thick blue velvet darkness.

The road which led up from the tavernas divided after about fifty yards. One branch went straight up the hillside, the other took a more oblique route. Ginnie indicated the second with her torch. 'We'll go this way. Not so steep.'

It was still quite a marked incline, and Mrs Pargeter started to puff a little as she pulled her substantial bulk upwards. At a point where the track turned sharply, she stopped for a breather and looked back. Pinpricks of stars in the sky and dots of light from boats gleamed back at her. Then, over the sea, sudden triangles of light raked out across the water from the further shore.

Ginnie turned back at that moment and her torch found Mrs Pargeter's puzzled face. 'Searchlights from Albania,' she explained.

'Really?'

'Oh yes. They come on most nights.'

'What are they looking for?'

The outline of Ginnie's shoulders shrugged against

the night sky. 'No idea. Nobody knows much about what goes on in that place. Come on. Not far now.'

'Right.' Mrs Pargeter readdressed herself to the steep track of broken white stone. 'It's times like this that I really am determined to lose some weight.'

But it was said more for form than anything else. Mrs Pargeter lived at peace in her plump body. Her outline had always been generous and, as she grew older, that generosity had begun to verge on prodigality. But the late Mr Pargeter had never complained. Nor had anyone else, come to that.

She saw a tiny spot of light appear suddenly and move in a hazy scribble above the scrub to the side of the path. As suddenly it disappeared. Then another showed. And another.

'What on earth are those, Ginnie? I don't think I believe in fairies.'

'They're fireflies.'

'Really? God, this place is so beautiful, isn't it?'

'So beautiful,' Joyce echoed. Then her voice was broken by a sob. 'What a beautiful place to be alone in.'

'You're not alone, Joyce. I'm with you.'

'I know, Melita, but . . .' More sobs came. 'I mean, Chris isn't here. Chris'll never be anywhere again. I don't think I can manage without him.'

'Of course you can. It'll take time, but you'll do it, Joyce. That's what Chris would want you to do.'

'Oh God, Chris wanted me to do so many things. Even now he still wants me to do things. He's left me a letter with great lists of instructions. I just don't think I can cope.'

'You can cope. You'll—'

Mrs Pargeter stopped at the sound of a door closing ahead and hurrying footsteps approaching. The beam of Ginnie's torch moved up from the ground and briefly illuminated the impassive face of the young woman from

Spiro's kitchen as she almost ran towards them.

'*Kalinikta, Theodosia*,' the rep said.

Without any response, the woman pushed past them and, using the direct path which their curving one had now rejoined, hurried on down the hillside.

Mrs Pargeter flashed a look across to Joyce, to see if the silent Greek woman's appearance had repeated its traumatic effect, but her friend just looked weepy and preoccupied.

'What have you done to offend her?' Mrs Pargeter asked Ginnie.

'Nothing. Theodosia can't speak. She's dumb.'

'What? But—'

'Here we are – the Villa Eleni.' Ginnie accompanied the interruption with a sweep of her torch across the frontage of the building ahead of them. A low white-painted rectangle with a shaded veranda at the front. Under this, either side of a front door, were double French windows, closed in by louvred shutters.

'She could have left a light on,' muttered Ginnie.

'Who?'

'Theodosia.'

'You mean she had just come from here?'

'Yes, she was checking it was tidy before you came in.'

'I'm sorry? I don't understand.'

'Theodosia is the maid for the Villa Eleni,' Ginnie explained patiently. 'She's Spiro's sister, you see, and he owns the place.'

'Oh, does he?'

Ginnie pushed open the unlocked door and switched on some lights, illuminating a central living area. A couple of wicker armchairs were placed near the entrance and at the far end, by the doors leading to the kitchen and bathroom, were a dining-room table and chairs. The bedrooms ran the length of the building, one each side of the central area. Ginnie opened the windows and shutters at each end of Mrs Pargeter's room. 'Sea view at the front, and at the back you get a lovely outlook on to the garden.'

Mrs Pargeter joined her on the low balcony at the back of the bedroom. Light spilled on to flowers and shrubs in pale-blue-painted oil-drums.

'Can't see much in this light,' Ginnie apologised, 'but you wait till morning. The flowers are really fabulous this time of year.'

'I look forward to it,' Mrs Pargeter said.

She gazed back into the bedroom with satisfaction, approving the neat twin beds with their white sheets, the functional wooden bedside furniture, the gleaming marble floor. Though self-catering was not her usual style, this really could have been a lot worse. Not lavish, but comfortable and well-maintained. Yes, if she could only manage to cheer Joyce up a little, she was set for a very enjoyable fortnight.

When Mrs Pargeter and Ginnie went back into the living-room, there was no sign of Joyce, but the sound of running water could be heard from the bathroom.

'Well . . . if you've got everything you want,' the rep said, 'I'll be off.'

'It all looks fine, thank you. Very comfortable.'

'You'll find there are sort of basic supplies in the fridge. We always stock our clients up with a bit of food and a couple of bottles of wine. Or there's mineral water if you want something non-alcoholic. That's probably safer than the tap water.'

'Mineral water'll be fine. I feel quite parched.'

'Yes, everyone gets dehydrated in this heat. You must make sure you keep up your fluid intake. Would you like me to get you a glass of mineral water now?' asked Ginnie, suddenly solicitous.

'No, no, I'll manage.'

'Right. As I say, it'll be in the fridge. Now, what else should I tell you . . . ? The minimarket opens at nine in the morning, and fresh bread's delivered there round nine thirty. Spiro'll change travellers' cheques, or you can do them at the Hotel Nausica – though Spiro's rate tends to be better. I'll be in the taverna between twelve and one tomorrow, if there's anything you want to check with me, and emergency numbers are in the villa guide on the table over there.'

'Thank you.'

'Well, I hope you'll be comfortable . . .'

'Sure we will be.' Mrs Pargeter, hostesslike in her new home, held the door open for her guest. 'You have far to go, do you?'

'Not far,' Ginnie replied uninformatively.

'Well, goodnight.'

'Goodnight.'

The rep did not bother to switch on her torch, the path familiar to her from many such visits. Soon her outline vanished into the darkness. Mrs Pargeter watched a couple of fireflies ignite and extinguish themselves, then closed the door.

She checked the contents of the fridge and found them more lavish than she had expected. Bread, cheese, jam, some ham and sausage. Long-life milk, a couple of bottles of white wine, the promised mineral water. And a bottle of ouzo.

For a moment she contemplated hiding this, but decided that she couldn't. Joyce might have seen it, for one thing, and she was a grown woman, after all. If she really was going to be helped out of her current state, the approach must be cautious and tentative. But Mrs Pargeter felt quietly confident that, with the unforced help of the sun and the sea, she could achieve much for her friend in two weeks of gentle therapy.

She poured herself a large glass from the square plastic bottle of mineral water and went through to her bedroom to unpack. The cases, she noted with satisfaction, had been delivered to the right rooms. In fact, apart from the delay at Gatwick – a circumstance beyond the tour operators' control – all of the arrangements had been commendably efficient. She heaved a suitcase up on to one of the beds and put the key into its padlock.

It was at that moment she realised, with annoyance, that she had left her flightbag down at Spiro's. She remembered taking it off the coach and putting it under her seat at the taverna. Then, in the confusion of Joyce's sickness and their hurried departure, she had left it there.

Oh well, never mind. Her flightbag always contained toothbrush, face-cloth and make-up in case of airport delays, but she had others in her main luggage. Passport, credit cards and travellers' cheques were in her handbag which she had with her, so at least her valuables were safe. And, Mrs Pargeter thought as she stifled a yawn, she certainly didn't fancy walking down that steep path and back up again.

No, the flightbag would come to no harm overnight. She'd pick it up in the morning. And, even if it did get stolen . . . well, that would be a nuisance rather than a disaster.

She heard movement from the living-room and went through to see what state Joyce was in.

The answer, immediately apparent, was not a very good state. Joyce, hair wet from the shower, sat at the table, with a dressing-gown wrapped around her, facing two glasses and the ouzo bottle from the kitchen. One of the glasses contained clear water, the other already showed the clouded white of diluted ouzo.

'I really wouldn't have any more of that, Joyce. It made you sick last time.'

'It wasn't that that made me sick,' came the belligerent reply.

'What was it then?' asked Mrs Pargeter lightly.

'It was . . . It was . . .' For a moment Joyce hovered

on the brink of replying, but caution reasserted itself. 'Anyway, why're you telling me what I should do?'

'I'm not. I'm just suggesting—'

'Yes, you are!' Joyce bawled back. 'No one lets me lead my own bloody life. All the time we were married, Chris kept telling me what to do. And he's still telling me what to do from beyond the grave. And now Conchita tells me what to do and you tell me what to do and—'

'What do you mean about Chris telling you what to do from beyond the grave?'

'I mean . . .' Again Joyce teetered on the brink of confession, and again drew back from the edge. 'I know what I mean. That's all that matters. It's none of your business, Melita.'

'Very well, if you say so.'

Suddenly Joyce stated to weep. 'Oh, Melita, Melita . . . Everything's such a mess. I can't do it.'

'Can't do what?'

'Can't do anything. Can't do what Chris wants me to do. Don't even really know *what* he wants me to do, but he's got my curiosity aroused and I can't just do nothing . . .'

'Chris is dead, Joyce. He can't make any further demands on you.'

There was a bitter laugh. 'Don't you believe it.'

'Listen—'

But Joyce was in no mood for listening. No, Mrs Pargeter feared, if anyone was cast in the listening rôle that night, she had drawn the short straw. Normally she wouldn't have minded, but that particular night she did feel so tired. So exceptionally tired. She raised her hand to mask another yawn.

But the long night's listening never materialised, because it soon became apparent that Joyce was at least as tired as she was. The sobbing and the maudlin recrimination were quickly swamped by yawns and, within half an hour, it required only the minimum of persuasion to get her friend into bed. Joyce insisted on having the ouzo bottle and a glass on the bedside table beside her, but, even before her light had been switched off, she was fast asleep.

And, within five minutes, so was Mrs Pargeter.

8

Mrs Pargeter opened her eyes and blinked at the bright parallelogram of light on the white wall opposite. She had not expected to sleep through. Usually she took a night or two to settle into a new bed.

Still, there was no doubting it was morning. She felt rested, though a little headachey. Perhaps she just wasn't used to the retsina . . . Mind you, she hadn't had that much of it. The second half-litre bottle had not been touched, and she hadn't mixed it with anything else. She shared the late Mr Pargeter's views on the subject of Greek brandy and had never liked the aniseed taste of ouzo.

Her head still felt muzzy when she stood upright and wrapped round her blue cotton dressing-gown. Already the air felt warm in the bedroom.

She moved to the front windows. The shutters and tall glass doors were pinned back, the view obscured by gauzy curtains which bellied and slackened restlessly in the sea breeze.

Mrs Pargeter pushed through them to the white glare of the sun, which challenged her aching head. But when her eyes accommodated to the brightness, the beauty of the scene melted away all thoughts of pain.

The tops of olive trees and cypresses shielded the sea frontage of Agios Nikitas from view, and Mrs Pargeter looked straight out across to the blurred outline of Albania. The sea was of that uniform blue that one distrusts in travel brochures, its surface raked here and there by the lazy swirls of currents. A large cruise ship slid sedately across the centre of the channel. The white sails of a yacht flotilla moved like formation seagulls over the blue. Nearer to the coast, awning-topped motorboats puttered along, searching for those secret bays which were rediscovered every day by new pioneers. A speedboat, planing high out of the water, towed behind it the white smudge of a waterskier.

Yes, thought Mrs Pargeter, I am going to like it here.

As she turned back into the villa, her shadow crossed a basking lizard which flicked out of sight, a black comma instantly erased from the whiteness of the wall.

She moved through the bedroom to the back windows, whose translucent curtains strained outwards into the garden. Once through them, she stood on the little balcony, looking out on a scene perhaps more beautiful than that at the front.

The flowers glowed in reds, mauves, blues, pinks and yellows against the dusty green of their leaves. All were neatly trimmed and tended, many rising from cans and drums painted in a powdery blue. The pots nearest the villa, still shaded by the building's edge, were circled with dampness. The white cement pathways had been punctiliously brushed. Whoever kept the garden in such a pristine state had already completed that morning's servicing.

As she looked at the display, Mrs Pargeter wished she knew more about flowers. She had always liked having a nice garden to walk in, but never taken much interest in how gardens got to be nice places to walk in. Nor had the late Mr Pargeter had 'green fingers' (other adjectives had been applied to his fingers with some frequency, but never 'green'). However, when they lived in the big house in Chigwell, there had always been a continuing supply of labour to look after the grounds. The men who came to stay had all been happy to pay with weeding and digging for the privilege of a few days' invisibility behind the garden's high walls.

But, as she looked at the splendour of that array of Corfiot blooms, Mrs Pargeter wished she had had a little more 'hands-on' experience of horticulture. It would be nice to be able to give names to the flowers. She felt pretty confident about the geraniums, both the red and pink varieties, and would have been prepared to risk identification of the climbing plant with cornet-shaped blooms of bright blue as Morning Glory, but the rest stumped her completely.

Pretty, though. She could recognise that. They were all very pretty.

Distressing, she thought with mild regret, that there weren't any better words to mean 'pretty'. Always sounded so limp. Particularly when applied to a woman. 'Oh, she's very *pretty*' – huh, talk about damning with faint praise. Almost as bad as calling a man 'sweet'.

Mrs Pargeter grinned at the way her thoughts were flowing. When irrelevant ideas started to interconnect in her mind like that, it was always a sign that she was beginning to relax. Not bad, really, one night in Corfu and already the therapy was taking effect.

Yes, one long, relaxed night in Corfu. Her headache had gone now. How long *had* she slept? For the first time that morning she looked at her watch.

Good heavens! A quarter to twelve. It was years since she'd slept that long. Something in the Corfiot air perhaps?

She moved out of the shadow of the balcony and stood there, blinking, letting the sunlight wash over her. Soon she would have to have a shower, get dressed . . . what then? Wander down to Spiro's to pick up her flightbag, mustn't forget that. Have some lunch there too, maybe. (Mrs Pargeter had already firmly decided that, though the package had been described as 'self-catering', breakfast would be the only meal prepared in the villa. And, if she was going to wake this late every morning, she didn't think breakfast would figure very large in her daily schedule.)

She wondered if Joyce was up yet. Had her friend slept equally well, or been kept awake by her troubled thoughts? There was no sound from the other bedroom. Perhaps she'd already gone out. Down to the minimarket, maybe even to one of the beaches for a swim. If Joyce was doing things on her own, that was good. The two of them might have come on holiday together, but both had agreed that they didn't want to live in each other's pockets.

Mrs Pargeter looked idly down at the white cement path and saw that she was causing a traffic hazard. One of her plump bare feet was blocking the advance of a file of tiny ants. With uncomplaining efficiency, they had made a detour, circling the obstruction and then continuing their column in a perfectly straight line.

Amazing organisation and discipline you have to have to be an ant. Amazing ability to sublimate your own personality to that of the community. Wouldn't suit me, thought Mrs Pargeter.

She watched where the line of ants was going. The file moved, relentlessly regular, along the path towards the villa. Then, making no concession to the change of plane, it continued vertically up the wall on to Joyce's balcony.

Mrs Pargeter moved forward and saw how the line progressed across the marble platform and under the billowing curtains into the bedroom. Intrigued, she followed them, wondering what attraction prompted this dedicated troop movement. And, come to that, why there was no returning line of ants.

Inside the room her questions were answered. The single line of ants stopped by the side of the nearer bed, where it joined a mass, an orgiastic mêlée of other ants.

Ants gorging themselves on the browning pool of blood that disfigured the spotless marble floor.

Other ants had climbed up the brown-stained sheet which dangled off the side of the bed. They moved in hungry confusion over the white crumpled linen.

And over Joyce Dover's equally white, equally crumpled body.

And ants seethed round the dried-up gash on her wrist, through which Joyce Dover's lifeblood had flowed away.

9

Mrs Pargeter moved out on to the balcony and took a long series of deep breaths. The innocent scent of flowers in her nostrils felt obscenely inappropriate. Life with the late Mr Pargeter had trained her well in coping with shock, but she had still been profoundly shaken by what she had seen. She swallowed back nausea, forced herself into a straitjacket of calm, took one more deep breath, and went back into Joyce's room.

The only way, she knew, was to dissociate herself, depersonalise what she saw, imagine that she had to examine the scene for some kind of test, that questions would be asked later. Horror can only be borne if one ceases to think of the individual identity of those involved; too much compassion can be crippling. All carers – doctors, policemen, ambulancemen – learn to cope by manufacturing a professional distance between themselves and the disasters they face.

As she had this thought, Mrs Pargeter realised that the necessity for distance applied equally to murderers, rapists and other violent criminals. It is only when one has ceased to think of people as individuals that one can perpetrate such horrific abuse to their bodies.

She looked down at the corpse. Thinking of it as 'the corpse' helped. The corpse, the deceased, the victim, the body . . . any word was better than a proper name.

The weapon which had severed the body's radial artery was plain to see. It lay on the floor, thickly streaked with brown blood and a volatile speckling of ants. The bottom of a broken ouzo bottle, a misshapen tumbler with one side rising to a deadly pinnacle of glass. It was the bottle that the deceased had insisted on having at her bedside the night before.

Easily done, Mrs Pargeter supposed – the contents drained, the bottle smashed, then one quick drunken slash across the wrist, rewarded by the welcoming embrace of oblivion.

She bent down close to the body's drained lips. Yes, there was an unmistakable smell of aniseed. The pillow, though dry, gave off a hint of the same perfume. Some of the ouzo – only a little, though – had been spilled.

Mrs Pargeter moved round the bedroom, sniffing, but nowhere else could she smell it. Presumably the deceased had consumed the entire contents of the bottle.

There was a wicker wastepaper basket by the dressing-table; inside it Mrs Pargeter saw shards of glass and the torn ouzo label. An uncharacteristically tidy gesture for someone about to commit suicide, she mused.

Not all the glass had gone into the wastepaper basket; there were a few tiny crystals and splinters on the marble floor nearby. She looked closely at the wall above the basket. On the white emulsion there were clear outlines of a few flat mosquitoes, swatted with paperbacks no doubt by previous tenants of the room. There was also, nearly three feet above the ground, a small arc-shaped indentation, from which a shiny trickle of dried fluid descended. She put her face close to the wall and once again smelt a nuance of aniseed. It seemed a reasonable deduction that the ouzo bottle had been smashed against the wall there.

Mrs Pargeter stood still, obscurely troubled. She looked across at the inanimate heap on the bed and thought for a moment.

Then she left the bedroom and went into the kitchen. She sniffed round the sink, but there was nothing to arouse her suspicions. She opened a drawer and found it to be well-stocked with cutlery, including two substantial and very sharp kitchen knives.

She closed the drawer and moved on to the bathroom. The ceramic base of the shower and its drainage outlet were completely dry. So was the washbasin, but from its plughole emanated the faint, unmistakable whiff of ouzo.

Mrs Pargeter stopped for a moment to assess this information and work out a possible scenario of events during the night.

The deceased had woken in the small hours, depressed and suicidal in the emptiness of her bereavement. She had drunk more ouzo to try and shift the mood, but the alcohol had only deepened her despair. She had decided to kill herself.

Up until that point the scenario was just about credible. The next bit of reconstruction, however, made it less convincing.

In her drunken and self-destructive state, the deceased had looked for a suitable means of suicide. Rejecting – or perhaps unaware of – the possibilities of the kitchen knives, she had decided to use glass from the broken bottle to cut her wrist.

But there was still some ouzo left. Rather than drinking it up or just letting it spill over the floor when she broke the bottle, the deceased had gone to the bathroom and emptied the residue into the wash basin. She had then gone back into her bedroom and smashed the bottle against the wall, considerately ensuring that most of the glass would fall into the wastepaper basket. Her suicide weapon thus neatly created, the deceased had meekly got back into bed, slashed her wrist with the vicious spike of glass, and slipped quietly out of existence.

Mrs Pargeter's credulity felt strained.

Any other scenario, though, did have considerable ramifications.

Like, for instance, the involvement of another person.

Suppose, Mrs Pargeter conjectured, another person had been involved . . . ? Suppose the deceased had not moved from her bed, but the other person had drained the ouzo bottle, smashed it and slashed the deceased's wrist . . . ?

A lot more details fitted into that scenario.

It raised certain new problems, though. Chief among them was why the deceased had not resisted the attack on her. She might have been asleep at the moment of assault, but the cutting of her wrist must have wakened her. Surely she would have screamed or . . . ? Surely Mrs Pargeter would have heard something . . . ?

But Mrs Pargeter had heard nothing. She had slept very deeply. Quite exceptionally deeply.

A new thought struck her, a thought which might explain both her own exceptionally deep sleep and the passivity of the deceased.

She moved quickly from the bathroom to the kitchen. She opened the fridge. Almost everything that had been there the night before was still there. Bread, cheese, jam, ham, sausage, long-life milk, the bottles of white wine. Only two items were missing.

She knew what had happened to the bottle of ouzo.

But where was the square plastic bottle of mineral water?

She searched through the kitchen. She looked in the waste-bin outside the kitchen door. She searched her own room. Keeping her eyes averted from the sheet-shrouded body, she searched the other bedroom. She searched the living-room and the bathroom.

The bottle of mineral water had disappeared. Its contents could not be checked for the powerful soporific she now felt sure it had contained. In just the same way that it would be hard to trace the drug in the ouzo which had rendered Joyce so pathetically unresistant to her fate.

Joyce. For the first time since seeing the body she had let herself think of her friend once again as a person. Mrs Pargeter caught sight of her face in the bathroom mirror and saw the tears begin to flow.

And she determined from that moment that she would find out who was responsible for this ultimate depersonalisation of her friend.

Because Mrs Pargeter knew now that she was dealing, not with a suicide, but a murder.

10

In the confusion of the night before, Mrs Pargeter had not unpacked her suitcases, but that morning the minute she opened the first one she knew that someone had been through them. Everyone has their own style of packing and, although her possessions had been punctiliously replaced, tiny details – a silk sleeve folded too tight on its tissue paper, a pair of sandals too accurately aligned – betrayed the intervention of an alien hand.

So while Mrs Pargeter had been unconscious, someone, confident of the sleeping drug's efficacy, had calmly searched her belongings. The knowledge gave her an unwholesome, tainted feeling, almost as disturbing as the shock of what had happened to Joyce.

Mrs Pargeter went through to the other bedroom and checked the suitcases. Her friend, she knew, was an untidy packer, but the neatness with which her clothes had been laid out confirmed the unsurprising truth that Joyce's possessions had also been examined.

For a moment Mrs Pargeter wondered whether the search might have been the main purpose of their nocturnal visitation. Was it possible that Joyce had woken, seen a stranger going through her belongings, and been killed merely to prevent her from identifying the intruder . . . ?

But no, that didn't work. The circumstances of the murder, its disguise as suicide, suggested a degree of premeditation which was at odds with that scenario.

Mrs Pargeter felt certain that whoever had entered the Villa Eleni during the night had intended to kill Joyce. And also to find something that Joyce had brought with her to Corfu. Whether the murderer had been successful in the second part of his or her mission, there was no way of knowing.

Mrs Pargeter was grimly thoughtful as she dressed. She would have liked to take a shower, but didn't want to risk disturbing any evidence. Though uncertain how sophisticated forensic investigation would prove to be on Corfu, she knew that the less she touched the better. It went against her notions of hygiene, particularly after the sweatiness of the long day before, but, in the cause of criminal investigation, she confined her toilette to copious applications of deodorant and Obsession.

She couldn't even use mineral water to clean her teeth, so she forced the toothpaste round with her tongue. Fortunately, she always kept a little breath-spray in her handbag, and a couple of puffs from that gave her the confidence to go out and speak to people.

She did one more slow circuit of the villa, to check that she hadn't missed anything. She gazed for a long, sad moment at Joyce's body, which seemed distanced and shrunken in death. Then she looked outside at the front and back for signs of the murderer. Entering the premises would have presented no problem – in a climate like that, French windows were almost always left open at night – so she had no hopes for signs of forcible entry, but there was a distant possibility of a footprint in the dust or sand.

Nothing. Whoever had tended the garden had swept the cement paths too diligently for any trace to remain. That of course raised the question of who the careful gardener was. Had the watering and sweeping been part of some regular daily routine, or were they done that morning on special orders? As he or she swept, had the gardener been aware of the horror that lay a few yards away, hidden only by flimsy net curtains?

Such questions would have to be asked. And answered. But, Mrs Pargeter told herself firmly, they were questions for the Corfiot police. Though the tragedy came so close, there was no reason for her to become involved in its investigation.

She tried to clamp a lid firmly down on the seething broth of inconsistencies and possibilities that boiled inside her mind, and set off to report a death.

Almost directly overhead now, the midday sun was ferocious and enervating, but the direct track to Spiro's did not seem so steep as it had the night before. Partly, of course, that was because Mrs Pargeter was going down rather than up, but, as she looked across in the daylight at the other, curving path she had taken with Joyce and Ginnie, the longer route appeared to be at least as steep and, here and there, even steeper.

Mrs Pargeter crammed the lid firmly down on that speculation too.

The taverna was open, but there were not many customers. It was not yet one o'clock, and the lunchtime trade wouldn't really get going for another hour. The Secretary with Short Bleached Hair and the Secretary with Long Bleached Hair sat over glasses of Sprite. Both wore bikinis that constricted their plump flesh like rubber bands; and already their white curves blushed from incautious exposure to the Mediterranean sun. They were engaging in a little come-hither banter with the beautiful Yianni, who was being polite, though clearly uninterested, as he swept round the tables with a broom made of bunches of twigs.

At another table sat Ginnie, doing her promised problem-solving stint. Mr and Mrs Safari Suit, dressed exactly as they had been the day before, were the ones with problems, and they appeared to be bending the rep's ears unmercifully. Ginnie, Mrs Pargeter noticed with interest, had a scratch on her face and the beginnings of a black eye, which had not been there the night before. On that detail too Mrs Pargeter did not allow herself to speculate.

She looked cautiously towards the table where she and Joyce had sat. It was on the edge of the eating area and had not yet been reached by Yianni's broom. She saw with relief that the flightbag still remained under her seat. Casually, she moved across, as if to look out over the bay, and picked it up.

She had not yet decided who should be the first recipient of her dreadful news. The person she wanted to tell was Larry Lambeth. He was the most sympathetic contact she had on Corfu and she needed to share some of the emotions building up inside her. Also, his background would make him a useful sounding-board for conjecture about the crime.

But this was a murder case and protocol must be observed. The local police should be notified as soon as possible. (Mrs Pargeter had always been a great believer in keeping the police supplied with as much information as she reckoned they could cope with.) Spiro was the one with a telephone, so presumably at some point he must be involved in contacting the police, but Mrs Pargeter decided that Ginnie should be the one to know first of Joyce Dover's death.

Mr and Mrs Safari Suit, however, appeared to be settled in for a long session of complaint. 'I mean, the brochure,' Mr Safari Suit was saying, 'didn't indicate that the Villa Ariadne was so far up the hill, and it's not as if my wife doesn't have her varicose veins to contend with. I really think the tour operator should move us into another villa nearer to sea level and my wife and I are also very disappointed that the crockery supplied in the . . .'

If ever Mrs Pargeter had had news that would justify breaking into a conversation, now was that moment, but it was not her style to create unnecessary shock and distress. No, she would bide her time, wait until Ginnie was free, and then break the news to her discreetly.

So she sat down at an adjacent table, ordered a coffee from Yianni (a Nescafé – she couldn't take that gravelly, sweet Greek stuff), and waited.

Mr Safari Suit went on at inordinate length, but eventually, unable to think of anything else to complain about, set off to take some photographs of Mrs Safari Suit against a background of fishing boats.

Mrs Pargeter moved across to the next table and Ginnie gave her the professional smile of someone who had just coped with one whingeing nit-picker and is fully prepared to face another. 'No major problem, I hope?' she asked breezily.

'Well, yes, I'm afraid there is. It's Joyce.'

'Oh dear. Still unwell, is she?'

'Rather worse than unwell, Ginnie. Joyce is dead.'

'What?' There was a fraction of a second's pause. 'Oh no. That's the holiday rep's nightmare. I've been lucky, I've never had one of my clients die on me before. Oh, how dreadful. What happened?'

It was what had happened in the pause after Ginnie had said 'What?' that interested Mrs Pargeter. There had been a grinding gear-change in the girl's reaction, and after that gear-change she had been back in control. She had responded with appropriate concern and, if that concern had been selfish rather than compassionate, it had still been the proper response of a professional faced with a professional problem.

But her first reaction, the one expressed in that almost breathless 'What?', had been one of naked fear.

The fear of someone who had just had her worst imaginings realised.

11

Mrs Pargeter did not use the word 'murder'. She just described, as impassively as she could manage, the scene that she had encountered in Joyce's bedroom.

Ginnie, whose professional control had firmly reasserted itself after that one brief lapse, nodded grimly. 'I'll see that the proper authorities are notified,' she said, and disappeared into the taverna, instructing Mrs Pargeter to wait for her. The rep was gone for some time.

The area under the awning started to fill up with minimally-clad tourists, the level of whose tans showed, to the precise day, how far they were into their fortnight's packages. Drinks were ordered, then the waiters came with their paper tablecloth routine, and plates of food started to appear.

Mrs Pargeter didn't feel hungry, and thought that it might be quite a while before she ever felt hungry again. She ordered a bottle of retsina from Yianni, but the wine tasted metallic and emetic on her tongue, so after a few sips she gave up.

Meanwhile, in spite of the iron discipline she was trying to impose on herself, thoughts continued to seethe and bubble up in her mind.

Ginnie came back after half an hour, accompanied by Spiro. His eyes were even darker with concern, as he sat down beside Mrs Pargeter. 'I am so sorry, lady, for what has happened. It is very sad, your friend, very sad.'

'Yes.'

'The police will be along to the villa soon, Mrs Pargeter,' said Ginnie. 'Obviously there's no way the other holidaymakers aren't going to find out what has happened eventually, but I'd be grateful if you could keep quiet about the death for as long as possible.'

'That goes without saying.'

The rep picked up her shoulder-bag. 'I must go back to the office in Corfu Town. There's going to be a lot to sort out, informing next-of-kin, that kind of thing.'

'Joyce just had the one daughter. Conchita. I think I've probably got her address somewhere if . . .'

Mrs Pargeter was saved the trouble of riffling through her handbag. 'It's all right. We'll have all the details in the office.'

'Oh, very well.'

'Are you sure you're all right, Mrs Pargeter? I mean, I could easily call a doctor if you want some sedation or . . .'

Sedation is the last thing I want after the night I've just had, thought Mrs Pargeter, but all she said was, 'No, I'll be fine, thank you.'

'Spiro will keep an eye on you. Won't you?'

'Of course, Tchinnie. Will you have something to eat, please?'

It was interesting, Mrs Pargeter noticed as she refused Spiro's offer, that the Greeks couldn't pronounce the 'J' sound at the beginning of 'Ginnie'. The consonant came out as a kind of 'Tch'. 'Tchinnie'.

'Mrs Pargeter, obviously you won't want to stay in the Villa Eleni . . .'

'I hadn't really thought about that, Ginnie. I mean, I don't mind. I'm not squeamish.'

'I was thinking maybe you'd want to go straight back to England?'

Oh no, not yet. Mrs Pargeter was very firm in her mind about that. She wanted to wait at least until the police investigation was under way. She wanted to be sure that her friend's murder was getting the attention it deserved. And if it wasn't, she didn't rule out the possibility of doing a little mild investigating herself.

In which event, she would be well advised to stay at the Villa Eleni. Murders are much easier to investigate if you're actually on the scene of the crime.

'No, I think I'll stay around for a while,' she said coolly. 'Probably find it easier to relax and get over it out here than back in England.'

'Very well, if that's what you feel. I'll arrange to book you into the Hotel Nausica and have your belongings moved there.'

'I'd think I'd rather stay in the villa.'

'That would not be appropriate,' said Ginnie firmly.

'No,' Spiro endorsed. 'The police will want as little disturbance as possible. They will need to do very thorough investigation of this suicide.'

Well, it won't be thorough enough if they start from the premise that the death was suicide, thought Mrs Pargeter, but all she said was, 'I should think having my bags moved to the hotel would cause quite a bit of disturbance.'

'That will of course be done under police supervision,' said Ginnie. She looked at her watch. 'I'll ring through now to sort out the hotel, and get a message to you there when I know how long your bags will take.'

'Thank you. I can manage overnight with what I've got here, if necessary.' Mrs Pargeter tapped her flightbag. As she did so, she remembered what else it contained. Yes, she looked forward to opening the package that Joyce had given her at Gatwick.

'Good' said Ginnie. 'There'll be no problem with the hotel – they're not fully booked – so you can go up there as soon as you like. Spiro'll show you the way.'

'Of course. I drive you if you want.'

'That's very kind.'

'Right, I'll go and sort things out,' said Ginnie, unable to erase from her voice all traces of resentment at the inconvenience she was being put to. Then she disappeared into the taverna to phone the hotel.

'Very sad,' said Spiro, his melancholy black eyes moist with compassion. 'Sad when someone feels so bad to do this to themself.'

'Yes, if that's what happened . . .' Mrs Pargeter hazarded.

Spiro looked shocked. 'What you mean – *if* that is what happened?'

She shrugged. 'Well, I'm sure the police will find out the truth.'

'Of course. Yes, of course.'

They seemed to have run out of conversation. 'Look,

I'll be fine, Spiro. I'm sure you should be getting on. You've got lots of customers.'

'No problem. The boys can deal with them. No, you have had shock. I stay talk with you.'

'Very well. Thank you.'

Though no doubt kindly meant, this solicitude was the last thing Mrs Pargeter required. All she really wanted was to be left on her own. To give her thoughts a chance to organise themselves. Maybe to go back up to the Villa Eleni for another look round. Certainly to investigate the package in her flightbag.

Still, if she was going to be stuck with him, she'd have to make some conversational effort. 'There seem to be a lot of people on Corfu called Spiro,' she began safely.

'Oh yes. It is the name of our saint. Saint Spiridon. You can still see his bones in Corfu Town if you want to.'

'Thank you very much.'

'He has been good for our island, so many men are called Spiros. First son often called Spiros. My father Spiros – I Spiros – if I had a son, he would be called Spiros.'

Mrs Pargeter looked out over the tranquil harbour and wished that this conscientious nursemaid would leave her to her own devices.

'Very sad,' said Spiro, returning to an earlier theme. 'Very sad for someone to kill themself. Your friend, Tchinnie say, lose her husband not long ago . . . ?'

'Yes.'

'Very sad, death of someone close. I know. My brother die, my father die. When something like that happen, people go a little crazy.'

'Yes.'

'They crazy – they think they can't go on – they kill themself – no problem.'

'Well, it is a bit of a problem for those who are left behind.'

'Yes, of course. I mean, no problem for them to do it. It seems the right thing to do – if you are a little crazy.'

'Perhaps.'

The conversation had once again trickled away, but Spiro showed no signs of leaving, so Mrs Pargeter moved on to another safe topic. 'You do speak very good English.'

'Thank you. You own taverna, you have speak English. So many English people come on holiday.' A gloomy shadow crossed his face. 'Not so many this year. Number of visitors down this year. But you have to speak English all the same.'

'Did you learn English at school?'

'A little. But it was not my best. Science best . . . chemistry and so on.'

'And did you continue your studies after school?'

He shrugged. 'Not possible. I leave school early. My father die, I have to take over taverna. Family business more important than school.'

'Ah. Do you ever regret you couldn't go on with your education?'

He was a little affronted by this question and answered defensively, 'Taverna is a good business. Good business for last twenty years with many tourists. Not so good last two years, but good business.'

'Yes. Yes, of course.' Mrs Pargeter decided to make use of the subject, since it had come up. 'And you say the taverna's a family business?'

'Of course.'

'So everyone working here is related?'

'Yes. Cousins, nephews, so on. All related.'

'And it's your sister who works in the kitchen, isn't it? Theodosia?'

For the first time in their conversation, he was on his guard. 'Yes, it is my sister.'

'But she doesn't speak?'

'No, she cannot. From a child, she cannot. You like some food now?' he went on, changing the subject without any attempt at subtlety.

Mrs Pargeter was not to be deflected. 'Last night, as we were going up to the Villa Eleni, we met Theodosia leaving it and—'

Spiro looked across the tables and spotted someone he urgently had to greet. 'Excuse me, I see English friends from last year. Must say hello. You let me know when you want I drive you to hotel.'

'Oh, it's all right. The walk'll do me good. I could do with a bit of fresh air.'

Spiro was far too keen to get away to notice the incongruity of Mrs Pargeter's last sentence, spoken as it was by someone sitting out of doors. He scuttled off, arms bonhomously open.

The question about Theodosia had not been wasted. Though not yielding any information, it had at least got rid of Spiro.

Mrs Pargeter waved to Yianni, who refused to accept any money for her coffee and retsina. She wondered idly whether it would be added to her running total from the night before, or if Spiro had waived payment as a gesture of compassion.

Then she set off across the waterfront towards the Hotel Nausica, a pink, almost rectangular building which rose up out of the trees the other side of the bay.

She was half-way there before the thought struck her. Why shouldn't she go up to the Villa Eleni and have another look round? There was no one to stop her, and if anyone did make a fuss, she could say she just needed to pick up some of her belongings.

She took the direct path up the hillside. It was certainly no steeper than the other one, and a lot shorter. She was hardly out of breath at all when she reached the front door of the villa.

She went in that way, ignoring the open French windows on either side. There was no reason for her approach to look surreptitious.

As soon as she was inside, Mrs Pargeter sensed that she was not alone. Silently, she moved through into Joyce's bedroom.

A tall man in uniform stood there, facing the far window. He turned at the sound of her entrance. In his gloved hands, he held the bloody bottle end which had slashed Joyce Dover's wrist.

It was Sergeant Karaskakis.

12

'What are you doing here?' His English was heavily-accented but precise. Cold and efficient, like his small dark eyes and that triangle of black moustache. Mrs Pargeter was forcibly reminded of the last time she had seen Joyce and Sergeant Karaskakis together, and of her friend's shocked reaction to the sight of him.

'Well, I'm staying here, aren't I?' she replied pugnaciously. She sensed that the Sergeant was trying to overawe her, and Mrs Pargeter had always been very resistant to being overawed.

'I understood you were being transferred to the hotel.'

'Well, yes, I am, but I remembered something I wanted to pick up here.'

'You should not have come in. The villa is closed during police investigations.'

'And is that what you are involved in at the moment, Sergeant?'

'I beg your pardon?'

'Police investigations? I always understood that nothing should be moved at the scene of a crime.'

He looked down at the murderous piece of glass in his gloved hands. 'I am a police officer. I am entitled to examine the premises.'

'But you're Tourist Police,' Mrs Pargeter insisted. 'I didn't know that violent deaths in Greece were investigated by the Tourist Police.'

'Of course they are not,' Sergeant Karaskakis said tetchily. 'I am merely having a preliminary look round. Then I will report back and officers from the relevant department will take over.'

'And will the "officers from the relevant department" be pleased to know that you have moved some of the evidence?'

Her words had the effect of making him put the piece of glass back down on the floor, but there was no apology in his voice as he said, 'This is not your business.'

'I'd say it was very much my business. It's my friend who's dead.'

'Yes, and of course I am very sorry about this. It is unfortunate for you at the beginning of your holiday. Also unfortunate for us. It is not good that people bring their troubles out here and do things like this. It makes for complications. Death always makes for complications.'

Mrs Pargeter didn't disagree.

'I suppose,' the Sergeant went on, 'that you will be returning to England now as soon as possible – yes?'

'Well, no,' Mrs Pargeter replied firmly. 'I've decided I'm going to stay for a while.'

'I don't think there is much point in that. You will

not enjoy your holiday after this tragedy. It is better you should go home.'

The final suggestion was spoken with the force of an order. As ever, such an approach only made Mrs Pargeter dig her toes in more firmly. 'I don't want to go home until I'm confident that Joyce's death is being properly investigated.'

Sergeant Karaskakis bridled at this implied criticism of Corfiot police procedure. 'The proper investigations will of course take place. I was only thinking from your point of view. For you to be too involved can only be painful. What I am proposing is that you should make a statement about how you found your friend dead, about the state of mind she was in, and then you would be free to go home. The other tedious details could be sorted out without you.'

'Which tedious details?'

'Organising the return of the body, that kind of thing. Don't worry, it can all be done very discreetly.'

'Swept under the carpet, you mean?'

'I'm sorry, I do not understand. What have carpets to do with this?'

'I mean, "hushed up". You want to have Joyce's death hushed up, don't you, Sergeant?'

'That is not so unusual. It is for her family. Very few people want a great deal of publicity about a suicide.'

'I don't think Joyce's death was suicide,' said Mrs Pargeter quietly.

This really did shake him. 'What! But it is obvious. Her husband has just died, she is in a very bad state, she kills herself.'

'She didn't leave a note.'

'Maybe not. We don't know yet. Perhaps we will find one. Anyway, she told people the bad state she was in. Ginnie heard her talking about it.'

That had been rather quick, thought Mrs Pargeter,

for Sergeant Karaskakis to have had time to discuss the case with Ginnie.

'Of course she committed suicide.' His voice had now taken on a bullying note.

But Mrs Pargeter was impervious. The late Mr Pargeter had told her how few bullies can cope with having their bluff called. Ignoring their threats completely was the course of action he always recommended. And he did know – rather well – what he was talking about.

'I am convinced,' said Mrs Pargeter quietly, 'that Joyce Dover was murdered.'

'Don't be ridiculous!' Now the Sergeant was really angry. 'You say things like that, you make trouble for everyone. A murder investigation causes great disturbance. You don't want that – particularly when there is no murder to investigate,' he added as an afterthought.

'I know she was murdered,' Mrs Pargeter persisted, 'and nothing you say will convince me otherwise. What is more, I am going to stay here in Corfu until the person who killed her is brought to justice.'

Sergeant Karaskakis gave her a stern, cold stare. 'You are being very foolish. You do not know how much trouble your stupid attitude will cause. This is not your country. You do not understand how things work out here.'

'I understand how justice works, and I thought that was meant to be universal. Don't you have justice out here?' she asked in deliberately infuriating mock-innocence.

'Yes, of course we do! And of course this death will be properly investigated. But it will be more easily investigated without your interference.' His voice took on a softer, more cunning note. 'Anyway, what is it that makes you think your friend was murdered?'

'Various things.'

'What things?'

'I will tell that to the appropriate investigating authorities,' Mrs Pargeter replied.

He was stung by the answer, as she had meant him to be. 'You will regret this stupidity.'

'Why?'

'You will regret it because, if you insist on calling the death murder, you automatically become a suspect.'

'I don't see why.'

'But it is obvious. You were here in the villa last night. You came out from England with Joyce Dover. She knew no one in Corfu. It is generally found that murders are committed by people known to their victims.'

'All right. So I become a suspect. That doesn't worry me, because I know I'm innocent.'

'You could still have a very inconvenient time during the investigation until you are *proved* to be innocent.'

'That's a risk I'm prepared to take.'

'You would not be allowed to leave the island. You would have to hand over your passport until the investigation was over. That could take months.'

'There's nothing I've got to rush back for,' said Mrs Pargeter with infuriating calm.

Sergeant Karaskakis made one more attempt to frighten her. 'You will only be making trouble for yourself. You would do better to mind your own business and return to England straight away. Otherwise I am afraid you might regret it.'

But Mrs Pargeter didn't frighten that easily. She smiled a sweet smile and, at least for the time being, Sergeant Karaskakis knew he was beaten.

13

The Hotel Nausica wasn't Mrs Pargeter's idea of a hotel, but then she had been rather spoiled in such matters by the late Mr Pargeter. It was clean, though, and the tracksuited black-haired girl who greeted her in American English was friendly. So long as she didn't think of it as a hotel, but as a taverna with rooms above, Mrs Pargeter reckoned it would be fine.

Her second-floor bedroom was almost identical to the one at the Villa Eleni, though it only had French windows and shutters one end. These gave out on to a small balcony, with a lounger on which one could lie and look out over the perfect stillness of the bay.

'Is there anything I can get for you?' asked the girl.

'No, I don't think so, thank you very much. My bags will be coming over at some point, so if they could be brought up when they do arrive . . .'

'Sure.'

'Your English is very good – or should I say your American?'

'Oh, thank you. Actually I'm studying at Boston University. Psychology.'

'Ah. And you're just over here for the summer?'

'Yes. My father owns the hotel.'

'I see. Can I ask what your name is?'

'Maria.' The girl hovered in the doorway. 'If you're sure there's nothing you need . . .'

'No. Oh, one thing . . .'

'Yes?'

'I might need to use a telephone. Is it true that Spiro's taverna's got the only one in the village?'

Maria grinned wryly. 'Did Spiro tell you that?'

'No.'

'You surprise me. It's the sort of thing he does. Sharp businessman, old Spiro. Tells tourists they can only cash travellers' cheques with him, only hire cars and boats through him, only use his telephone . . .'

'So there is another one?'

'Here in the hotel. Just say when you want to use it.'

'Thank you. Am I to gather that there's a bit of rivalry between Spiro and the Hotel Nausica?'

'Just a bit.' Maria shrugged. 'Always rivalries on Corfu. Most have been going on for generations. Family arguments over who had the right to certain olive trees, that kind of thing. Tourist trade just provided a new battleground for the old rivalries.'

'I see you have lots of opportunities for applying your psychology out here . . .' said Mrs Pargeter mischievously.

The girl grinned. 'Yeah. Quite a culture shock coming back here after Boston.'

'I'm sure. Very different societies.'

'You can say that again. Takes a bit of adjustment sometimes. I mean, I love Corfu, but there are things like . . . well, the attitude to women, the expectations of women . . . ' A wry shake of the head.

'Not at the sharp end of the feminist movement?'

Maria grimaced. 'That is something of an understatement. You should just hear the wails of disappointment when some poor woman has the nerve to give birth to a girl.'

'But there are shrieks of delight when it's a boy?'

'You said it.'

'You said,' Mrs Pargeter began, taking advantage of their new intimacy, 'that most of the rivalries out here were family rivalries. Do you mean that your father is related to Spiro?'

'Oh, certainly,' Maria replied with a laugh. 'Everyone in Agios Nikitas is related to everyone else. My father and Spiro are cousins – not first cousins but some sort of cousin. Everyone comes from the same town, you see – Agralias.'

'So they're not from Agios Nikitas originally?'

'No – or yes. Let me explain. Agralias is about five miles inland from here. That is where everyone still has their main home. But many people from Agralias also own a bit of land on the coast, plots that have been in their families for years. Suddenly, when the tourist boom started, those bits of land on the coast became very valuable.'

'So people built tavernas . . . ?'

'Sure. Tavernas, villas, shops, hotels . . .'

'And it was good business?'

'Oh yes. If you owned a taverna in the early years you could do very well indeed. Well by Corfiot standards, anyway. Before the tourists came, it was pretty much a peasant economy here, you know.'

'Yes. I see. That's explained a lot. Thank you.'

'No problem.' Maria thickened her accent, parodying the Corfiot catch-phrase. She moved out into the corridor. 'So, if there's anything you want, just say . . .'

Mrs Pargeter waited five minutes to make sure that the girl had really gone and, even then, opened the bedroom door again to check. Feeling ridiculously surreptitious, she went out through the French windows to ascertain that she couldn't be overlooked from another balcony. The scene that greeted her was as idyllically innocuous as ever. Unless Albanian spies had superpowered binoculars trained on her, she could feel confident that she was unobserved.

She sat on the side of the bed and unzipped her flightbag.

The package which Joyce had entrusted to her at Gatwick Airport was just as she had remembered it.

Under the brown paper and cardboard wrapping was an irregular rectangle, the glugging of whose contents suggested some kind of bottle.

When first handed over, the package's significance had seemed minimal, at worst perhaps a symptom of the seriousness of her friend's drinking problem.

But when Joyce's prognostication had been proved correct by the Customs search of her luggage at Corfu Airport, the potential significance of the package had grown. (As Mrs Pargeter had this thought, she was reminded of the striking likeness she had noted between the Customs officer and Sergeant Karaskakis. Given what Maria had just told her, it would perhaps not be fanciful to guess at some family connection between the two men.)

Now that Joyce had been murdered by someone who had searched her belongings in the Villa Eleni, the package she so carefully offloaded on to her friend had become extremely significant.

The paper had been roughly secured with a couple of strips of Sellotape. Mrs Pargeter broke these and reached into the cardboard sleeve to pull out its contents.

She didn't know precisely what she had been expecting, but certainly not what she found.

The package contained a bottle of ouzo.

A decorative bottle of ouzo, fashioned in the shape of a Greek column. The kind of souvenir that is available at every airport shop and supermarket in Greece.

Now, Mrs Pargeter could just about imagine that someone with a drinking problem might suffer from a paranoid fear of running out and carry emergency supplies . . . But why ouzo?

And why take ouzo bought in England into Corfu, where it's available at a fraction of the price?

That really was coals to Newcastle, thought Mrs Pargeter.

14

'So far as I can gather,' said Mrs Pargeter, 'Joyce didn't know anyone out here. She wanted to go to Greece because she'd never been there with Chris, so it wouldn't raise painful memories. Having made that decision, she just trotted down to her local travel agent and asked what was available. They recommended this package, and that's how we ended up in Agios Nikitas.'

Larry Lambeth tapped his teeth pensively. 'You're sure she didn't say anything which now, like with hindsight, might make you think she had got some connection out here?'

Mrs Pargeter shook her head. 'I'm positive she didn't say anything. The only detail that could suggest a connection is the strange way she reacted when she saw Sergeant Karaskakis. And when she saw the girl, Theodosia. I suppose she might have met one of them before in England.'

'It's just possible that Sergeant Karaskakis has been abroad, but I'm sure Theodosia never has. Very unlikely ever to have left Corfu, particularly with her not being able to speak and that.'

'Hm.' Musing, Mrs Pargeter looked out from the terrace of Larry Lambeth's villa towards the sea. The Mediterranean night had just fallen with its customary suddenness, and the lights of Albania once again twinkled mysteriously over the water.

The villa was set in a hillside olive grove, about three miles from the coast. It was an older building than the mushroom developments of Agios Nikitas, with floors of comfortingly worn stone. The terrace was peaceful under its awning of woven bamboo, and the night air seemed to have released the perfume of the surrounding trees. Every now and then a distant donkey let out an affronted bray.

After opening Joyce's package, Mrs Pargeter had enjoyed an overdue shower and then rung Larry Lambeth from the hotel. He had instantly invited her out to the villa. Over retsina and brandy she had brought him up to date with Joyce's death and the events which had followed it.

Then they had sat down to a dinner of herb-scented lamb stew, served by a very pretty dark woman with a shy smile. Whether this woman had a role in Larry's life beyond that of cook was hard to guess. Though the direction of her smile occasionally hinted intimacy, she was not invited to join them at the table and he certainly seemed to treat her like a servant. But then, from what Mrs Pargeter had seen in the twenty-four hours she had been on the island, that was how most Corfiot men treated their womenfolk.

It always made her slightly cross to see a woman undervalued. Though Mrs Pargeter was no feminist, and had no wish to challenge for the traditional territories of male dominance, she was a great believer in equality within relationships. But then, of course, she had been rather spoiled by her life with the late Mr Pargeter.

'No, I think,' she continued, 'that the reason behind Joyce's death lies in the past. In her life in England, not out here.'

'You don't think it could have been just, like, a robbery that gone wrong? You know, some local lad breaks into the Villa Eleni, looking for cash, cameras, jewellery, that kind of stuff – Joyce wakes up – he tops her . . . ?'

'If you're doing that, why bother to make it look like suicide?'

'That's a point.'

'And, anyway, is there that much burglary out here?'

'Very little actually. Very little of the ordinary sort, anyway. Fact is, most people out here've got some connection with the tourist business. They know thieving and that's only going to put the punters off, so they make sure it doesn't happen.'

Something in his tone had alerted Mrs Pargeter. 'You say "very little burglary of the *ordinary* sort", Larry . . . ?'

'Yeah, well . . .' He gave a little, modest smile. 'Well, yeah . . . Like I said, I got a bit of a business going on my own account.'

'Yes?'

'Fact is . . .' He still looked sheepishly proud of himself. 'Fact is, as you know, when I worked for Mr P.—'

'My husband never spoke to me about the details of his work.' The temperature of Mrs Pargeter's voice had dropped by a sudden ten degrees.

'No, but, like, I was always good on the old documents. Need some papers nicked, need them fixed, arranged, emended, like . . . Larry Lambeth's the bloke you want – that's what Mr P. always said.'

Mrs Pargeter was more concerned about another of her husband's dicta. 'What you are ignorant of, Melita my love, you cannot stand up in court and talk about. I am very proud to be the husband of a woman who has never broken the law or been the possessor of any information about anyone else who might have broken the law.' The late Mr Pargeter had often said that to her.

She smiled at Larry Lambeth in innocent puzzlement. 'I'm sorry. I'm afraid I don't know what you're talking about.'

'OK, well, look, like coming up to date . . . Fact is, when I come out here, I got quite a stash. Bought the villa, no problem, still had plenty of drax left to keep me in the style to what I had accustomed myself. But – I'm not the first to do it and I know I won't be the last – I didn't take inflation into account, did I?'

'Ah.'

'So, anyway, after a few years, the old mazooma's getting a bit tight, and I start thinking to myself, like, maybe I better get something else going. Well, I don't want to go, like, back into the old full-time racket, do I?'

'I wouldn't know,' said Mrs Pargeter with a sweet-little-old-lady smile.

'No, right. Well, fact is, I definitely don't want nothing full-time, but I think to myself, like, I got these talents with the old documents and that – why don't I use them? And then I remember that the one thing that's always had a good international resale value – whatever the economic climate – is the old British passport.'

'What, so you mean you forge passports?' Mrs Pargeter's voice was suitable cowed by the shock of the idea.

'Not forge the whole lot, no – that's like a big job. No, I just, like, get the passports and then I doctor them.'

'When you say you . . . *get* the passports . . . ?'

'Well, this is why it's magic being out here, isn't it?'

'I don't know what you mean.'

'Look, Mrs P., lots of English punters come out here, don't they?'

'Certainly.'

'Well, first couple of days they're very good about things . . . put their cash in money-belts, take their passports and valuables with them at all times, close all the shutters, lock up the old villa every time they go out . . .'

'Yes.'

'But after that first couple of days, the old Corfiot bit gets to them.'

'The old Corfiot bit?'

'Sure, they *relax*, don't they?'

'Ah.'

'Place is famous for it. As a matter of fact . . . ' Larry Lambeth looked rather sedate for a moment. 'You heard of Mr Gladstone?'

'Mr Gladstone? Which Mr Gladstone?'

'The one what was Prime Minister.'

'Oh yes. Of course I've heard of him,' said Mrs Pargeter through her surprise.

'Well, he was out here for a while, you know, and he said he had "never witnessed such complete and contented idleness as at Corfu".' Larry Lambeth enunciated the quotation with a gravity befitting its provenance.

'Really? I didn't know that.' Mrs Pargeter was impressed. 'You're very well-read, Larry.'

'Yeah. Sure.' He looked a bit sheepish. 'Actually, I only read that in a holiday brochure.'

'Never mind. It's still very interesting.'

'Right. Anyway, so what I'm saying is . . . once the holidaymakers start to relax, start leaving the old villa windows open and that . . . well, it's dead easy for anyone who wants to go in and nick the odd passport, isn't it?'

'And that's what you do? That's the business you've built up?'

Larry Lambeth looked suitably pleased with himself. 'Yeah, right. Found a decent little gap in the market there. Ticking over quite nicely, thanks.'

'So you just steal any passports you happen to come across?'

He was affronted. 'No, come on, give me a bit of credit. It's not a random business, highly sophisticated operation, mine. Anyway, if I took too many, it'd start to look suspicious. No, mostly I'm working on commissions.'

'Commissions?'

'Sure. Someone says to me something like – I need a passport for a man in his sixties, five foot eight, fourteen stone, balding, white hair. So then I go along the beaches till I see someone who more or less looks like that, find out where they're staying, nick the passport.'

'But surely it gets reported as missing and then if anyone else tries to use it they get arrested?'

'Oh yeah, of course you have to make the odd adjustment to the document . . . change the number, the name, fiddle with the photo, that kind of stuff. But in my experience' – he gave the side of his nose a professional tap – ' . . . the less you have to change the better.'

'So who do you get your commissions from?'

'Varies a lot. Most of my business, though, comes through Hamish Ramon Henriques.'

'Who?'

'Come on, you must know Hamish Ramon Henriques. Mr P. was working with him all the time.'

The frost returned to Mrs Pargeter's voice. 'As I said, I knew very little abut my late husband's work.'

'Oh yeah. Right. Well, Hamish Ramon Henriques is, like, a travel agent. Rather specialist travel agent, I do have to say. But, anyway, I get a nice lot of commissions through him. He gives me the details of what he's looking for . . . I find it, do the necessary doctoring . . . send it back to him. Nice, neat business, sweet as a nut. Incidentally' – he leant towards Mrs Pargeter in a confidential manner – ' . . . if *you* ever find yourself wanting a false passport, you have only to say the word.'

'That's extremely kind of you,' said Mrs Pargeter primly, 'but I think it very unlikely that that situation will ever arise.'

'Mrs P., as the cyclist said before he drove into the bus – you never know what's round the next corner.'

'No, that's very true. You don't.'

Larry Lambeth suddenly barked out some instructions in Greek and the pretty woman appeared with a basket of peaches and black cherries. She got no word of thanks as she put it down on the table, but once again the way she looked at Larry, her smile half-amused and half-insolent, suggested a closeness between them. Her task completed, she receded discreetly into the villa.

Larry bit into a peach and caught its trickling juice with his tongue. 'Anyway, sorry, got a bit side-tracked there. What we really should be doing, like, is finding out who done in your mate Joyce.'

'Yes.'

'And you reckon the reason behind it's something back in England?'

'I think it must be. At least there are certainly things I'd like to find out from England. Some information about Joyce's husband, for a start.'

'Well, pretty obvious what you got to do then, isn't it, Mrs P.?'

'What?'

Larry Lambeth looked at his watch. 'They're two hours back in England, so, yes, I'd say this was the perfect time to ring Truffler Mason, wouldn't you?'

'Yes,' said Mrs Pargeter. 'I think it well could be.'

15

'Hello. Mason de Vere Detective Agency.'

The voice, as ever, sounded as if it had just received information from an unimpeachable source that Armageddon had arrived.

'Truffler, it's Mrs Pargeter.'

'You don't know how good it is to hear from you.' The gloom in Truffler Mason's voice deepened. Not only was the world about to end; he'd also discovered that hell did exist and, what's more, it was compulsory.

Mrs Pargeter, who knew his manner of old, took the words at face value. 'Very sweet of you to say so. It's good to hear you too, Truffler.'

'Everything all right out there?' Anxiety joined the terminal depression in his voice. 'I hope Larry Lambeth made contact. I told him to keep an eye on you.'

'I'm calling from Larry's now. Thank you very much for setting that up.'

'Least I could do. When I think how your late husband looked after – no, nurtured, that's the word – when I think how your late husband *nurtured* me in my career . . . well, whatever I do for you's going to be too little.'

'Thank you very much,' said Mrs Pargeter at the end of this funeral oration. 'That's very sweet of you.'

'And you're having a good time? Everything all right, is it?'

'Oh yes, everything fine,' she replied automatically. Then, remembering, continued, 'Well, except for the fact that my friend's been murdered.'

'What!'

'My friend, Joyce Dover, who I came on this package with, was murdered last night. It was made to look like suicide, but there's no doubt it was murder.'

'I'll come out there straight away,' said Truffler with mournful determination.

'No, there's no need. I'm not in any danger.' Mrs Pargeter did not give herself time to question the truth of that assertion. 'You can be much more use to me in England. Listen, I want some investigation done into Joyce's background.'

'Fine. Give me the details.'

'Are you sure you've got time? There aren't other cases you should be getting on with?' A clattering and thumping was heard from the other end of the phone. 'Are you all right, Truffler? What was that noise?'

'Just me clearing my desk, Mrs Pargeter. From now on, your investigation is the only thing I'm working on.'

'But, Truffler, you shouldn't—'

'I know my priorities, thank you. Come on, tell me what you want found out.'

'All right. Well, really it's anything about Joyce Dover's background. And her husband's background, which, I've a feeling, is just as important. His name was Chris. He died a few months back, end of March I think it was. Anything you can get on either of them – particularly anything which might give them some kind of link with Corfu.

'OK. And what about his death?'

'What do you mean?'

'Want me to check that everything was kosher there? I mean, maybe there was something funny went on with him snuffing it. Murders do tend to breed murders,' Truffler Mason concluded lugubriously.

'Yes, you're right. That's a very good thought. As I recall, Chris died of a heart attack . . . or was it a brain tumour?'

'Heart attacks can be engineered easily enough.' Truffler Mason sounded as if he was speaking from gloomy experience.

'True. Yes, so anything you can find out on his death too. I don't know how long it'll take you, but—'

'Give me Joyce Dover's address and I'll call you tomorrow night. About nine. Where shall I get you – Larry's?'

'Erm, I'm not sure. Might be better at the hotel.'

'Which hotel's that?'

'Hotel Nausica. Agios Nikitas. I'm afraid I haven't got the number on me.'

'Don't worry, I'll get it.'

'Sorry to put you to the trouble.'

'Mrs Pargeter, compared to some of the things I've

had to find out in my time, dealing with International Directory Enquiries is a doddle.'

'Yes, I suppose so. I'll give you Joyce's address. And she has a daughter called Conchita. I'll give you hers too.' He took down the information. 'Truffler, I really am grateful to you.'

'It's nothing. Like I say, after the way your husband looked after me, anything you need, lady, you only have to say.'

'Oh.' Once again the reminder of the late Mr Pargeter's solicitude brought a moistness to his widow's eye. 'Well, bless you. And everything's going well for you, Truffler, is it?'

'Absolutely fine,' said Truffler Mason, in the voice of a man over whose head the hangman has just placed a bag.

16

'And anything I can do?' asked Larry, as he drove her gently over the broken rocks of the track down to Agios Nikitas.

'Well, there's lots of local stuff I need to know about. Sergeant Karaskakis, for instance, anything you can find out about him . . .'

'Sure.'

'I mean, presumably he's related to people round here?'

'Oh yes. Karaskakis is very much a local name. Lots of them in Agralias. He's probably some sort of cousin of Spiro and Theodosia and Georgio and that lot. Most people round here are.'

'Right.' Mrs Pargeter was thoughtful. 'There's certainly something sinister about him, but whether he's criminal or not I don't know. His insistence that Joyce committed suicide could be just because he's not very bright and has gone for the obvious . . . . Or it could be because he doesn't want all the fuss of a murder enquiry – you know, anything for a quiet life.'

'Or that he thinks a murder enquiry wouldn't do the tourist trade a lot of good, so it's better hushed up.'

'Yes, hadn't thought of that one, Larry. Alternatively, he could be part of a conspiracy to cover up the murder and pass it off as suicide. He might even have killed her himself. There is some connection between them. I still can't forget the way Joyce reacted when she first saw him.'

'No, that was spooky, wasn't it?'

'Yes. Well, any information you can find out about him . . .'

'Leave it with me. Anything else?'

'Let me think . . . Ooh – Ginnie . . .'

'What about her?'

'Just that she's one of the few people out here who has direct links with England. I'm not sure that she quite counts as a suspect . . . Or perhaps she should be . . . I don't know. She's not very keen on you, incidentally, Larry.'

'It's mutual.'

'What's she got against you?'

'Just that . . . well, none of them have got much time for me out here.'

'Why?'

'Because I'm an outsider who's moved in.'

'But you're not as much an outsider as the English tourists. You are Greek, after all.'

He laughed. 'Yes, but the tourists only come for the odd fortnight – I'm a fixture. Fact is, just being

Greek is not enough, anyway. It depends whereabouts in Greece you come from. In Agralias they're suspicious of people from the next village. All over the island you got feuds and vendettas that have been going on for yonks. Anyone who hasn't lived here all his life is automatically suspicious. Oh no, so far as Agios Nikitas is concerned, I'm definitely an outsider.'

'But I don't see why that should concern Ginnie. She's not a local either, is she?'

'She lives with one, though.'

'Does she?' asked Mrs Pargeter in surprise.

'Sure. Why do you think a nicely-brought-up English rose suddenly sets up home in Corfu?'

'I assumed it was just because she had a job out here. Pretty nice place for a girl to spend her summers, I'd have thought.'

'For a young girl, maybe. Ginnie's a bit long in the tooth for the carefree sun-and-sea existence.'

'Yes, I suppose she is.'

'Not that it's all that carefree an existence, anyway. Listening to endless English tourists whingeing about the fact that their drains are blocked or the minimarket doesn't stock the right brand of baked beans.'

'See what you mean. So who does Ginnie live with? Not Spiro surely?'

'No, no. Spiro hasn't got a woman. She lives with Georgio.'

'The balding bloke who's always in the taverna?'

'Right. Lazy bum. Spends his life giving Ginnie grief and knocking back Spiro's ouzo. Never seen him pay a single drachma for it either. But then of course he's another cousin, isn't he?'

This new piece of information explained quite a lot. Like the way Georgio had been tearing Ginnie off a strip in the taverna the night Joyce died. Possibly even why Ginnie's face had been bruised.

The cross-currents and interconnections between the people of Agios Nikitas got more complicated by the minute.

The evening was beautiful and Mrs Pargeter felt too overstimulated to go straight to bed, so she sat under the awning of the Hotel Nausica to drink a last half-litre of retsina.

She felt a degree of satisfaction. At least, through the good offices of Truffler Mason and Larry Lambeth, her own investigation into Joyce's death was under way.

It was the progress of the official investigation that worried her. The encounter with Sergeant Karaskakis had firmly suggested that the death would be tidied up as quickly as possible, regardless of the true facts of the case. And increasingly she felt that if such a whitewash were attempted, the entire population of Agios Nikitas would close ranks in a conspiracy of silence to protect the cover-up.

She hadn't got a lot to go on really, until her investigators reported back. All the details that had convinced her Joyce's death was murder were up at the Villa Eleni, and Mrs Pargeter had a nasty feeling that most of them would already have been removed.

No, unless the villa were subjected to a proper forensic examination, all the evidence she had became merely circumstantial.

Except for the ouzo bottle.

She looked across to a group of German tourists who were noisily drinking ouzo. She watched as a waiter brought new glasses. She watched as the drinkers diluted the clear spirit and watched as the liquid clouded.

Mrs Pargeter gulped down the remains of her glass, left the two-thirds that remained in the retsina bottle, and rushed up to her bedroom.

Her hands trembled with excitement as she unsnapped

the seal on the bottle so tastelessly disguised as a Grecian column.

A preliminary sniff confirmed her suspicion. No aniseed tang. The contents were completely odourless.

She poured some into a glass, and filled another glass from the washbasin tap. Gently she trickled water in to dilute the contents.

The liquid remained transparent. She poured in more water to make sure, but still there was not the slightest evidence of clouding.

Whatever Joyce Dover had brought to Corfu in that bottle, it wasn't ouzo.

17

Mrs Pargeter thought she was dreaming. The sound of aeroplanes filled her dream. World War Two aeroplanes. They hummed in the distance, throbbed as they drew closer, screamed as they came overhead, then screeched away into the distance. A few minutes later the pattern would be repeated; another aeroplane would roar past. She felt she should be standing on the bridge of a ship next to a duffel-coated Kenneth More.

But she wasn't. She appeared to be in her white bedroom at the Hotel Nausica in Agios Nikitas. And so far as she could tell, she was wide awake. She pinched herself. Her flesh felt plumply and reassuringly solid.

Slipping out from the single sheet under which she had slept, Mrs Pargeter went on to the balcony. The tranquil beauty of the morning greeted her, and for a moment she thought it really must have been a dream from which she had just woken. But, even as she had the thought, she became aware of a distant humming.

It grew in intensity. The sound was unmistakably that of an aeroplane, which built in volume until confirmed by the sight of an old heavy-bodied transport appearing in the sky low above the hotel roof. The engine noise reached a crescendo, then diminished as the plane changed direction and vanished round the contour of a headland.

As she put on a beige cotton dress and fixed a brightly coloured scarf at her neck, Mrs Pargeter tried to find a rational explanation for what was going on. Albania hadn't suddenly declared war on Greece, had it?

No, perhaps someone was making a film or a television series . . . ? Yes, that was much more likely. So many bizarre phenomena these days could be put down to the excesses of the entertainment industry.

She got the true explanation when she was outside under the hotel's awning having breakfast. Just as Maria was serving her with coffee and a bowl of yoghurt and honey, the plane – or perhaps another plane, it was hard to tell how many of them there were – repeated its impression of strafing the Hotel Nausica.

'What is it?' asked Mrs Pargeter. 'Someone making a movie?'

Maria grinned. 'No, no, they're fire-fighting.'

'What do you mean?'

'We get lots of fires out here – particularly when there's as little rain as there has been this year. Much of the island is difficult to reach for fire-engines, but the planes can get there.'

'So what do they do? Do they have big water-tanks?'

'That kind of idea, yes. They fly out over the sea, land on the water to fill up the tanks and then fly back to drop it on the fire.'

'Good heavens,' said Mrs Pargeter.

Maria shrugged. 'Don't knock it. It works.'

'Oh yes, I'm sure it does. It's just an unusual idea – well, unusual for someone used to the good old British fire-engine. What starts the fires, though? Is it tourists throwing away cigarettes, lighting barbecues, that kind of thing?'

'Some of it, yes.' The girl seemed for a moment undecided as to whether to continue, but went on, 'And there's a certain amount of arson.'

'Arson? By the tourists?'

'No, by people on the island.'

'Why? What for?'

'Feuds, that kind of thing. Or the people from one village will get jealous because another village is doing better out of the tourist industry.'

'Really?'

'It's happened quite a lot in the last few years, since the number of tourists has been going down. Look over there.' She pointed to the scrub-covered hillside, through which the dusty track from the main road wound down to the village. An area of perhaps half an acre in the middle of it was dark grey, bare of greenery, with only a few gnarled and blackened sticks left standing. 'That happened a couple of months back. Agios Nikitas did well for tourists last summer – compared to the rest of the island. Somebody tried to ensure that it wouldn't do so well this year.'

'And does anyone here know who did it?'

Maria nodded enigmatically. 'Oh, I should think so. These feuds go back a long way. No, the problem is not usually deciding who did it, but deciding what revenge should be taken against them.'

'So what kind of revenge is likely to be taken?'

'I don't know,' said Maria shortly, deciding she had perhaps already given away too much, and went back into the hotel.

Mrs Pargeter was once again struck by the gulf between

the bright smiling 'No Problem' tourist image of Corfu and the realities of life on the island.

She had almost given up when he answered the phone. He sounded drowsy and Mrs Pargeter couldn't quite remove from her mind the image of Larry lingering deliciously in bed with his shy-smiling Greek woman.

'Good morning, Mrs P. What can I do for you on this bright and sunny?'

'Well, first, thank you very much for your hospitality last night. It was a lovely evening.'

'My pleasure.'

'And, second, I wondered if you knew anyone on the island who could do a bit of chemical analysis for me?'

'What?'

She filled him in on what she had found out about Joyce's ouzo bottle. 'So I was wondering if you knew anyone who might be able to tell me what's in it?'

'I think you'd better let me have a look at it.'

'Oh?'

'Fact is, in my line of work – documents, passports, that kind of stuff – I deal with quite a lot of chemicals. Always possible I'd be able to recognise it straight away, or, failing that, I could run a few tests and find out what it is for you.'

'That'd be great. As I say, it doesn't smell of anything. I haven't actually tasted it yet, but—'

'And don't you try, Mrs Pargeter!'

'What, tasting it?'

'Right.'

'Why not?'

'Look, Joyce Dover was murdered. We don't know why, but one quite common motive for committing murder is to stop oneself from being murdered. Maybe what she'd got in that bottle was intended to help someone on his or her way to the undertaker.'

'Poison, you mean?'

'That's exactly what I mean, Mrs Pargeter.'

18

With all her lines played out, Mrs Pargeter felt there was little she could do but wait for bites, so after breakfast she decided she would investigate the local beach. The bay of Agios Nikitas itself was just a harbour, but over the next headland, she had been assured, was the delightful beach of Keratria.

Mrs Pargeter bought herself a large straw hat for the expedition, and felt like an intrepid Victorian tracking down the source of the Nile as she set off up the little track out of the village. Although it was not yet eleven o'clock, the sun seemed already to have been turned up to 'full', and she was glad of the protective tracery of olive branches above her head.

She enjoyed the walk. Though undeniably overweight for her height, Mrs Pargeter was not unfit. Indeed, she was in better condition than most women in their late sixties. This state had not been achieved, however, by the indignities of calorie-counting or prancing in leotards. Its provenance was good eating, good drinking and, it must be admitted, a degree of pampering. But the main source of her well-being was the fact that Mrs Pargeter felt at home – and even at peace – in her own body.

Keratria proved, as promised, a beautiful beach. At one end a simple concrete taverna offered bamboo-covered shade and refreshment, and a few villas spotted the shore-line woods. Under a beach umbrella a mahogany-skinned young man kept a desultory eye on piles of blue fabric-covered loungers, a line of orange pedalos and a stack of sailboards, whose vivid sails splashed the pebbles behind him. He'd done all right with the loungers, there were a couple of pedalos circling lazily out in the bay, but nobody seemed interested in hiring the sailboards. Too much like hard work, as the sun spread its hazy lethargy. The young man didn't appear to be troubled by his lack of business.

Mrs Pargeter recognised a few people on the beach. The renters of the villas of Agios Nikitas did not stray far; they soon homed in on favourite beaches and tavernas. Even those with hire-cars tended, after a couple of days of frizzling sightseeing, to settle down and use their expensively-hired vehicles only to save the quarter-mile walk to minimarket or beach.

She saw Keith and Linda and Craig from South Woodham Ferrers. Linda, wearing a bikini which advertised her decision not to worry about stretchmarks, was trying to interest Craig in building a tower of stones, while Keith pored over his calculator, working out how the cost of the kilo of plums they had bought from the mobile fruit van that morning compared to English prices. Every now and then he commented to Linda how sorry he felt for all those poor devils stuck back in the office.

Craig was finding stone architecture less than riveting. He tried pottering down to the sea, but soon subsided on to his bottom, crying that the stones hurt his feet. With a child that age, Mrs Pargeter thought, Keith and Linda should really have gone to the sandier west of the island. Still, Craig'd be all right if his parents bought him some plastic sandals. Give Keith something else to compare the prices of.

She nodded at them and, a little further along the beach, passed the Secretary with Short Bleached Hair and the Secretary with Long Bleached Hair. They were prone on loungers, Walkmans plugging out the reassuring susurration of the sea. Both that day wore bikinis apparently designed by the inventor of the garotte, but the skin of their shoulders and thighs testified to the outline of every garment they had worn over the last forty-eight hours. Thin strap-lines showed white in the middle of the pink bands left by wider straps, while the puce area which had been exposed all the time already bore the tell-tale white flaking that presaged the loss of a whole layer of skin.

Now, belatedly, they had started to baste each other with cream and oil, but the damage had already been done. They were both going to be very uncomfortable for a couple of days, in no state to enjoy the abandoned Greek dancing of the taverna party nights which they had been promising themselves. Mrs Pargeter felt a maternal urge to tell them just to keep out of the sun for a couple of days, but she knew it wasn't her place to say anything.

She moved a little further along the beach, took a towel out of her bag and laid it down on the stones. Then she slipped off the cotton dress to reveal a brightly printed bikini beneath. Hers was more substantial than those worn by the two secretaries, but made no attempt to hide her voluptuousness. Mrs Pargeter knew her skin to be smooth and unmarked, and people who found plumpness unattractive were under no obligation to look at her. 'My Goddess of Plenty', that was how the late Mr Pargeter had always referred to her, she remembered fondly as she stepped in sandalled feet down to the sea.

The water was deliciously warm and Mrs Pargeter, a strong swimmer, enjoyed its therapy for more than half an hour. Then she rubbed herself down with the towel and slipped her dress back on, confident that any damp patches would dry as she walked along to the taverna.

The menu at Keratria was remarkably similar to that at Spiro's (which in turn bore an uncanny resemblance to the one at the Hotel Nausica). The predictability of Greek taverna food was something that Mrs Pargeter always forgot until, two or three days into a holiday, she was forcibly reminded of it.

Still, it was healthy. And tasty. She had a plate of moussaka, a Greek salad and half a litre of retsina. Very pleasant. Again glad of the olive trees' shadow, she set off back to Agios Nikitas.

It was probably just perverseness that made Mrs Pargeter go back to the hotel via the Villa Eleni, but she wanted to see how efficiently the murder scene had been sealed off, pending police investigation.

The answer, she discovered with only the mildest of surprises, was that it hadn't been sealed off at all.

The shutters and windows at the front were open, their thin curtains shimmering a little in the light breeze.

The front door was also wide open. Mrs Pargeter walked in. The living-room looked immaculate, every surface gleaming, as if ready to welcome new tenants.

She heard a slight sloshing sound from the room that had been Joyce's and moved towards it. Through the crack by the door hinges she could see the maid Theodosia on the far side of the bed, her arms busily swishing an unseen mop across the marble floor.

Mrs Pargeter went into the room. Theodosia looked up and caught her eye, but only stopped for half a beat in her rhythmic floor-washing. The rest of the marble was still damp from her ministrations.

Mrs Pargeter moved round the foot of the two beds and looked at the patch of floor she had last seen hideously discoloured with her friend's blood. Nothing remained. She looked at the bucket into which Theodosia had wrung her mop, but the water showed no brown tinge. This was not the first clean-up of the murder scene, just a final spit-and-polish.

How very convenient, Mrs Pargeter found herself thinking, almost like the houseproud 'little woman' she had never been, how very convenient marble floors are. Household stains . . . jam, mud, tomato ketchup, even someone's lifeblood . . . all vanish with a few easy strokes of a wet mop. No mess, no fuss – make sure *you* choose a marble floor when you're next thinking of committing murder.

The detached cynicism of these thoughts pained her and Mrs Pargeter felt tears threaten. Again she caught Theodosia's eye and seemed for a moment to see in them a reflected pain. Oh, if only the woman could speak . . . It would be in Greek if she could, of course, but the words could be interpreted. Mrs Pargeter felt certain that Theodosia knew something about Joyce's murder. If only there were a way of extracting that information . . .

'What are you doing here?'

The voice was shrill with anger. Mrs Pargeter turned to face Ginnie. The bruising on the rep's face had subsided a little, but was still painfully evident.

'I thought I'd just come in to see how the police were getting on with their investigations.'

'As you can see, they've finished.'

'If they ever started.'

'I don't know what you mean.'

'I mean that Joyce Dover was murdered, but there seems a marked unwillingness for anyone out here to investigate that crime.'

Once again Mrs Pargeter saw the light of fear in Ginnie's eye, the same fear she had seen when she first told the girl of her friend's death.

'That's nonsense, Mrs Pargeter. Joyce Dover killed herself. *I* heard her say she couldn't cope since her husband's death, *you* heard her say it too. I'm sorry that the truth is so hard for you to accept, but I'm afraid you will just *have* to accept it.'

'No, I won't,' said Mrs Pargeter cheerfully.

'What do you mean?'

'I mean that if the proper authorities aren't going to investigate Joyce's murder, then I'll find out who killed her myself.'

'I think you'd be extremely foolish to pursue the matter, Mrs Pargeter. You could get yourself in a great deal of trouble if you—' Ginnie's manner suddenly changed as, her professional grin firmly in place, she turned to welcome Mr and Mrs Safari Suit, who had just walked into the room.

'Well, here you are. I think you'll find this villa is a lot more convenient for the shops and the beach.'

'Oh yes.' Mr Safari Suit nudged his wife. 'Won't have so much trouble with your varicose veins here, will you, love?' He then favoured Ginnie with one of his witticisms. 'Sorry I had to make a fuss, but at least my efforts haven't been in . . . *varicose vein*, have they?'

He laughed immoderately at this inept sally. Mrs Safari Suit also thought it pretty hilarious. Ginnie smiled weakly.

'But tell me,' Mr Safari Suit went on, emboldened by his own brilliance, 'how does this villa suddenly come to be free? Hasn't been any trouble here, has there?'

'Good heavens, no,' said the rep, her eyes daring Mrs Pargeter to disagree. 'Just happened to be free, that's all.'

Mrs Pargeter didn't contest it. No point in making Mr and Mrs Safari Suit feel uncomfortable. She had nothing against them – well, nothing if you excluded his jokes.

It was interesting, though. Not only had Joyce's murder been swept aside as a suicide; now Ginnie was even denying that the suicide had taken place.

Another thing was interesting, too. Mrs Pargeter had no doubt in her mind that, at the moment when Ginnie was interrupted by the entrance of Mr and Mrs Safari Suit, the rep had been threatening her.

19

'Basically,' Truffler Mason's despondent voice intoned from the other end of the phone, 'I can't find out anything about Chris Dover's life before he came to England.'

'Ah,' said Mrs Pargeter. She was standing in the reception area of the Hotel Nausica, at the only phone available to residents (or, quite possibly, the only phone in the hotel). There didn't seem to be many people about, but she still felt exposed. Next time she talked to Truffler, she would do it from Larry's. The sense of conspiracy around Agios Nikitas was strong, the feeling that everything anyone said or did was very quickly communicated along the local grapevine.

'I mean,' Truffler continued, 'obviously I haven't had a chance yet to get proper investigations going in Uruguay, and maybe I'll be able to unearth something through my contacts out there. But it does seem from all accounts that Chris Dover kept very quiet about his origins. In fact he seems to have worked hard on presenting himself as the perfect English gentleman. Uruguay was hardly ever mentioned.'

'Perhaps that was just because nobody was interested,' suggested Mrs Pargeter.

'What do you mean?'

'Well, you know how insular the English are. So far as most of them are concerned, a foreigner's a foreigner – doesn't matter where he comes from. They just about recognise the difference between a Frenchman and a

German, but when it comes to less well-known countries, so far as your average Englishman is concerned, they're pretty much interchangeable. I bet most people you stopped in the street in England couldn't even tell you where Uruguay is.'

'So what are you saying?'

'I'm saying that possibly at first Chris Dover talked about his former life, but when it became clear no one was interested, he gave up and decided if you can't beat them, join them. Perhaps presenting himself as English made things easier for business.'

'You could be right.'

'Oh, by they way, you didn't find out what his real name was, did you, Truffler?'

'No records of him ever being called anything other than Chris Dover.'

'Hm, doesn't sound very Uruguayan, does it? Not very Hispanic. Must've been made up. Probably,' Mrs Pargeter went on, suddenly remembering how Larry Lambeth had arrived at his surname, 'based on his port of entry into England.'

'Could be. Anyway, he seems to have arrived in London in the late Fifties. Difficult to find out much about the early years, but he must've got involved in the export business at some level. First time there's much about him is when he started up his own company in 1963.'

'And was his business always legitimate?'

'Well . . . ' Truffler paused ponderously. 'Certainly in recent years no problems. Pure as the driven snow. Reading between the lines, though, I'd have said his early dealings was a bit more dubious. Haven't got anything definite yet, but hints I've heard from people in the business suggest Chris Dover may have started out as a bit of a villain.'

'What, not violence? Not gang stuff?'

'No, no. More your sort of white-collar crime. Export

business, but it was what he was exporting that was interesting.'

'What was he exporting?'

'Arms, it seems.'

'Oh?'

'To Africa, mostly. Always some nice little war going on in Africa to keep up the demand, isn't there? Anyway, from what I can gather, that's what he was into in the early Sixties – exporting stuff whose paperwork might not bear too close an investigation.'

'Gun-running.'

'Always one to call a spade a spade, wasn't you, Mrs Pargeter? So, anyway, presumably he made a pile from that, which provided the capital when he started his company in 1963. From then on, though, as I say, all very respectable.'

'Yes, certainly Joyce always seemed the soul of respectability. One would never have imagined that her husband was involved in anything he shouldn't be.'

Mind you, thought Mrs Pargeter with a little inward smile, of course the same could be said of me.

'But, Truffler,' she went on, 'you didn't manage to find any connection between Chris Dover and Greece?'

'Absolutely none. Certainly had no business dealings with Greece. Didn't go there on holiday. So far as I can tell, he'd never been near the place.'

'Hm.' Mrs Pargeter mused for a moment. 'Incidentally, did you get in touch with the daughter?'

'Conchita? No. I tried, but I think you'll find it easier to contact her than I will.'

'What?'

'She's on her way out to Corfu. The grisly business of taking back her mother's body.'

'Ah.' Mrs Pargeter wondered whether that meant the suicide verdict had already been achieved and the cover-up completed. 'Right. Well, I'll look out for her. Do you think you're likely to find out much more about Chris Dover?'

'Well, Mrs Pargeter, I got a lot of enquiries out. Something unexpected might come in from one of them. Though, in my experience, when you get a case like this where someone's deliberately covered their tracks, if you don't get a lead early on, you ain't going to get one.'

'Right.'

'I've found out the name of a solicitor Chris Dover dealt with a lot. Mr Fisher-Metcalf. I'm going to try and get to see him. Maybe find out something there, but I'm not overoptimistic,' he concluded in the voice which had never been heard to sound even mildly optimistic, let alone *over*optimistic.

'And what about his death? Anything odd there?'

'I've checked with the hospital. And his family doctor. Nothing. It was a brain tumour. Difficult thing to engineer, a brain tumour. Not like a heart attack – that's easy.'

'Yes. Did he look ill . . . you know, in photographs?' Mrs Pargeter knew Truffler's *modus operandi*. His first action in investigation of anyone – alive or dead – was to get hold of photographs of the subject, and his skill in obtaining these was legendary.

'I don't know.'

'What do you mean?'

'It's a strange thing, Mrs Pargeter. I've done a lot of investigation on this and, do you know, as far as I can tell, not a single photograph of Chris Dover exists.'

'Really? But surely there must have been something round the house?'

Mrs Pargeter felt slightly guilty for having said that. Just slipped out. She was never one to pry into any of her helpers' methods of investigation, but she knew that Truffler would already have entered and searched the Dovers' home. Shouldn't have mentioned it, though, she reprimanded herself. Keeping in blissful ignorance of any dubious deeds that might be going on was a talent Mrs Pargeter had refined over the years, and she wondered for a moment whether perhaps she was losing the knack. Still, it had been quite a time since the late Mr Pargeter died. Maybe she was just out of practice.

Truffler seemed unaware of her lapse, anyway, so it didn't matter. 'No, there was nothing. Absolutely nothing. Not in the office, neither. Company photographs, company reports, lots of that stuff, but not one of them shows a photograph of Chris Dover. Almost like he had a phobia about being photographed. Odd, that, isn't it?'

'Yes,' said Mrs Pargeter thoughtfully. 'Very odd.'

20

As she put the phone down, Mrs Pargeter saw Maria lingering in the doorway that led to the hotel kitchen. How long the girl had been there, or how much of the telephone conversation she had overheard, was impossible to guess.

But she gave Mrs Pargeter a large, totally unsinister smile and said, 'There was a message for you about an hour ago. From someone who wondered if you could meet her at Spiro's at ten o'clock this evening.'

'Did she give a name?'

'Yes. Strange name. It sounded like . . . Conchita Dover?'

'Ah,' said Mrs Pargeter.

* * *

At first she didn't think the girl was there. Though Mrs Pargeter hadn't seen Conchita since she was a child and so didn't know exactly what to expect, there was no one under Spiro's striped awning who looked as if she had just arrived on the island, summoned by news of a dreadful tragedy. There were the usual loud groups of English, louder groups of Germans and a few Greeks, the last no doubt holidaying relatives of the management. They had all had a few rounds of drinks, their food orders were starting to arrive and everyone was very relaxed.

Mrs Pargeter looked round again and realised there was only one person it could be. A dark-haired girl, who at first glance she had taken for a local, was sitting alone at a table, chatting to Yianni. Of course, there are certain very distinctive types right through the Mediterranean, Mrs Pargeter reminded herself. It was the Spanish blood of her father's relatives, filtered through Uruguay, that made Conchita Dover look so at home in Agios Nikitas.

On closer examination, the girl did look a bit too soignée to be a local. The way her thick black hair had been cut indicated an urban sophistication, which was echoed in the expensively casual flow of her designer pyjama suit.

Mrs Pargeter approached her. 'It is Conchita, isn't it?'

Yianni fired off one of his devastating smiles and left them to get on with the business of introduction.

'I'm terribly sorry about what happened to Joyce, Conchita. "Sorry" sounds a wretchedly inadequate word in the circumstances, but you really do have my sympathy.'

'Thank you.' There was a hardness in the girl's black eyes. 'I wonder if she got what she really wanted.'

'I'm sorry?'

'Mother had been threatening suicide for years.'

'What, since your father died, you mean?'

'No, long before that. Practically since I can remember.

She always was a dreadful emotional manipulator. Suicide threats used to be her ultimate weapon.'

'Oh?' This was a new insight into Joyce Dover. Once again Mrs Pargeter was reminded how little she had really known her friend.

'Mind you, she'd cried wolf so often, I'd long ago ceased to listen. Overdid it this time, though, didn't she? Called her own bluff good and proper.'

'Well . . .'

'Anyway,' said Conchita, picking up her ouzo glass and taking a savage sip, 'I'm not going to let it get to me. Mummy tried to control me all the time she was alive and, if she thinks she can continue the process from beyond the grave, she can forget the idea!'

Only the rigidity of her jaw betrayed the effort with which Conchita was holding in her emotions.

'I think using suicide as an emotional lever is utterly pathetic,' she went on. 'I very much doubt whether Mummy really meant it to succeed. Probably just intended another "cry for help", but cocked it up. Presumably the idea, as ever, was just to make me feel guilty. Well, if that was the intention, it isn't going to succeed!'

Mrs Pargeter hadn't been prepared for this outburst of recrimination and adjusted the way she had proposed to talk to Conchita. She would hold back her suspicions about Joyce's death for a while. Spiro's taverna wasn't the place for revelations of the kind she had to make.

On the other hand, if Joyce did have a history of threatening to kill herself, that could only help what Mrs Pargeter was now convinced was an intention on Sergeant Karaskakis' part to cover up the murder as suicide.

'Whatever your mother's reasons for doing it,' she announced uncontroversially, 'it's still very sad. Any premature death, however it's caused, is sad.'

'Huh,' said Conchita.

Yianni pirouetted back towards their table. 'Please,

can I get you something, please?' he asked Mrs Pargeter.

She ordered retsina. Conchita asked for another ouzo. The girl watched the waiter's retreating hips, very much in the way that her mother had done only a few days before. Her thoughts on the subject seemed quite similar, too. 'He's very dishy,' she murmured.

Mrs Pargeter agreed.

'Be quite nice,' Conchita mused, 'to indulge in a purely physical relationship with someone like that. Someone who's just beautiful, someone who doesn't speak the language, who can only communicate with his body. I'm sick to death of men who can talk!'

'Ah?'

'The only reason men are able to talk, it seems to me, is so that they can bore you to tears with lies and recrimination and self-justification. God, men are so pathetic – don't you find that?'

Though this description certainly did not conform with Mrs Pargeter's experience of the male sex, she didn't want to stop Conchita's flow, so she contented herself with a non-committal 'Certainly a point of view.'

'There are supposed to be these men around who are caring and concerned and altruistic and thoughtful and don't spend all their time trying to screw you up, and all I can say is – I've never come across any of them. All the ones I meet are complete shits.'

'What about your father?' asked Mrs Pargeter diffidently. 'Did he fit into that category?'

Conchita Dover softened instantly. 'Ah, my father was something special. He was a very caring man.'

Mrs Pargeter had heard similar views over the years from many only daughters, girls who were more than a little in love with their fathers, and whose fathers, without raising the dramatic spectre of incest, did nothing to discourage such flattering attentions. It seemed more than likely that Conchita Dover's dissatisfaction with men as a sex arose from the inability of those she had met to measure up to the idolised Chris.

The strong element of sexual jealousy in her next words confirmed this impression. 'He was wasted on Mummy, of course. Kowtowed to her, put up with her moods, did everything she wanted, worshipped her. And she just took him for granted. When he died, I really couldn't believe how God had got it so wrong. She was the one who should have died, not him.'

'If that's what you feel,' Mrs Pargeter interposed gently, 'you could say that God's adjusted the balance now. Your mother's dead, too.'

This statement of fact seemed to shock Conchita out of her cynicism. 'Yes,' she said, 'yes,' and lapsed into silence.

'I was never lucky enough to meet your father . . .'

'No.'

'I don't even know what he looked like . . .' This didn't produce any reaction, so Mrs Pargeter added another prompt. 'Do you have a photograph of him by any chance?'

'No. No, Daddy would never have his photograph taken.' So Truffler's surmise had been correct. 'Because of the scarring on his face.'

'Oh? I didn't know about that.'

'His face was quite badly scarred. He'd lost a good few layers of skin. It made his features look all sort of smoothed out . . .'

'Do you know how it happened?'

'He never said, but I think it was when he was in Uruguay. Apparently he had political disagreements with the government out there, which was why he left. I think the scarring was probably the result of torture.'

'But he never actually said that?'

'No. He never talked about Uruguay at all. Whenever anyone asked him about his early life, he'd just change the subject, or say some things were better forgetten.'

'I see.' Mrs Pargeter took a sip of retsina. 'Have you had any contact with the authorities out here . . . you know, about when they're likely to release your mother's body?'

'The initial contact came through the British Consulate . . . that's how I first heard about . . . her death. They said certain formalities would have to be gone through . . . I suppose the local equivalent of an inquest . . . but they didn't seem to think it would take more than a few days.'

'Presumably they were only passing on what the Greek authorities had told them?'

'Presumably. They seemed a bit . . . sort of embarrassed about it. But then my mother liked embarrassing people,' Conchita added vindictively.

'Death's always embarrassing.'

'Yes. "SUICIDE IN HOLIDAY PARADISE" – not the kind of headline that the tour operators are really going to welcome, is it?'

'No.' Still Mrs Pargeter held back her knowledge of the true circumstances of Joyce Dover's death.

'Anyway, it was suggested that I should get out here as soon as possible. There'll be papers to sign and that kind of thing before the body can be flown back.'

'Of course. So, what . . . you wait till someone contacts you . . . ?'

'Mm. Some local police representative, I think. There was a message to say he would meet me here this evening.' Conchita scrabbled in her handbag. 'I've got the name somewhere here. It was . . .'

'Sergeant Karaskakis?' Mrs Pargeter supplied.

'Yes,' said Conchita. 'That's right.'

21

'Talk of the devil,' murmured Mrs Pargeter.

Sergeant Karaskakis looked more geometric than ever as he approached them. The horizontal line of his cap paralleled the right angles of his uniformed shoulders, and the triangle of its peak was an inverse reflection of his perfectly symmetrical moustache.

His mouth was set in a professional smile to greet Conchita. This paled a little when he saw Mrs Pargeter. The music blaring from the taverna's speakers changed. Bouzouki gave way to Beatles.

He gave Mrs Pargeter a curt nod and turned to Conchita. 'Miss Dover?'

'Yes.'

'I am Sergeant Karaskakis.'

'How do you do?'

'I am very sorry about the unfortunate circumstances which have brought you here, and I trust that your journey was not difficult.' This had the air of a sentence that he had practised.

'No. It was a scheduled flight. There were no delays.'

'Good.' The Sergeant seemed to have taken a decision to conduct the conversation as if Mrs Pargeter was not there. 'Everything is proceeding as quickly as possible with the formalities, Miss Dover. I am optimistic that it will all be concluded in two or three days.'

'Fine.'

'And then you will be free to make your melancholy way back to England with the body.' He seemed rather pleased with this sentence, as if it was another one he had worked at and polished with the help of a dictionary.

'Thank you. So . . . what happens? Do I just wait to hear from you?'

'I will keep you informed, of course. You are staying, I believe, in Costa's Apartments?'

'Yes, the tour company organised that for me.' Conchita suppressed a yawn and looked at her watch. The tensions of the last couple of days were catching up with her. 'I think, actually, if there isn't anything else, I'll get on up there. I'm pretty knackered.'

'Knackered?' Clearly Sergeant Karaskakis' precise textbook English didn't encompass the niceties of slang.

'Tired.'

'Ah, yes.'

'So if you'll excuse me . . . And Mrs Pargeter . . .'

'You have a good night's sleep, Conchita love.'

'Thank you.' The girl waved across to Yianni and mimed writing a bill.

'I hope,' said Sergeant Karaskakis formally, bringing out what appeared to be yet another prepared line, 'that you will be able to enjoy your stay in Agios Nikitas as much as the unhappy circumstances permit.'

'Thank you.' Conchita turned the full beam of her smile on Yianni. 'Just for two ouzos, please.'

'Yes, of course, please,' he said, blushing a little and fumbling with his notepad.

'Got a taste for ouzo, have you?' asked Mrs Pargeter. 'You been out in Greece before?'

'No, never,' Conchita replied. 'But I've had it in Greek restaurants in London, and my father always liked it.'

'Oh,' said Mrs Pargeter.

Conchita paid Yianni and gave him a substantial tip. In full consciousness of her sexuality, she flashed him a farewell smile, then picked up her handbag and rose. 'See you around then,' she said to Mrs Pargeter. 'And you know where to find me when you need to, Sergeant.'

'Of course.'

He rose politely to see her off, but then sank down

again and looked at Mrs Pargeter. An arrogant smile twitched beneath his moustache, as he spoke.

'You will gather there have been no problems about Mrs Dover's death.'

'Yet,' said Mrs Pargeter defiantly.

'There will not be any,' he countered confidently. 'When all the evidence points in one direction, only a perverse person would try to disprove what is obvious.'

'I can be very perverse.'

'You would be very foolish to be perverse in this case – though very soon it won't matter, anyway.'

'What do you mean?'

'In two – perhaps three – days, the authorities out here will be satisfied to release the body. After that, it will not matter what ridiculous allegations about murder are made. The case will be over.'

'Who are these authorities?' asked Mrs Pargeter.

'The details do not concern you. Rest assured, all enquiries are being made in the correct way.'

'You mean the authorities have all the relevant evidence?'

'They have photographs, samples and reports from the scene of the incident.'

'Whose reports?'

He could not resist a wolfish grin as he answered, 'Mine.'

'No one else's?'

'Of course. Reports from police detectives as well.' He paused for a moment, enjoying the scene. 'Police detectives who, as it happens, are good friends of mine. One is my cousin, as a matter of fact.'

Just as the Customs officer at Corfu Airport had been. Mrs Pargeter knew she was up against a brick wall. Sergeant Karaskakis had got the whole case sewn up. However impartial the investigating authorities might be, he had seen to it that they were only presented with his version of events. And of course a suicide verdict would be much tidier and less disruptive than one of murder.

He spread his hands wide in a gesture of mock-helplessness. 'No, I am afraid there is nothing can be done. In two, three days it will be official that Mrs Dover killed herself. Then no further enquiry will be possible.'

'I know she was murdered,' said Mrs Pargeter doggedly.

Sergeant Karaskakis shrugged. 'I don't think anyone is going to believe you unless you can produce some evidence. And,' he continued with relish, 'I don't think there's any evidence to be produced.'

'Not out here, perhaps.' Mrs Pargeter didn't really know why she said her next sentence; it just seemed the right thing at the time. 'But I can produce evidence in England that will prove Joyce Dover was murdered.'

She was bluffing, but the bluff worked. Sergeant Karaskakis blanched and said, 'But you will not be able to get to England to find it.'

'Why not? I can go back tomorrow. I know exactly what I'm looking for,' Mrs Pargeter improvised like mad to justify her new position.

'I don't think you can go back tomorrow.'

'Why not?'

'All the flights are fully booked.'

He was improvising too. Mrs Pargeter was encouraged. By pure chance, she had stumbled on something that had got the policeman worried. Maybe the solution to Joyce Dover's murder really did lie in England.

'I'll manage to get back,' she asserted coolly.

'No, you won't.'

'How can you stop me?'

'I can stop you by . . .' He thrashed around, desperate for an idea. It came. 'I can stop you,' he announced with sudden confidence, 'because the investigations into Mrs Dover's death are not yet complete. There is still the possibility, as you say, that it could have been murder. That possibility of course makes you a suspect. Which means that you will not be allowed to leave Corfu until the investigation is complete. And also means,' he continued triumphantly, 'that you must hand over your passport to me until the end of the investigation.'

Mrs Pargeter took the passport out of her handbag and handed it over. Being without it would be a nuisance, but a small price to pay for the incontestable look of guilt she had seen in Sergeant Karaskakis' eyes.

22

'Mrs Pargeter, it'd be no problem at all. I'd be delighted to do it for you.'

'Are you sure?'

'Believe me. Please believe me.' There was no doubting the sincerity in Larry Lambeth's voice. She had phoned him the second she'd got back to the Hotel Nausica and he had arrived within twenty minutes to drive her out to his villa. Neither had voiced the thought, but both felt safer away from the prying eyes and ears of Agios Nikitas.

The Greek woman with the shy smile had produced brandy and retsina and pistachio nuts on the verandah. The impression of intimacy in her relationship with Larry was endorsed by the skimpiness of the negligee she had on. But, as ever, she knew her place and quickly disappeared back inside the villa, leaving them to talk in private.

'Fact is,' Larry continued, 'you're doing me a favour.

After all Mr P. done for me, I've really been longing for the day when I could do something for you by way of return.'

'But you have done something for me. You've looked after me wonderfully since I've been out here.'

He dismissed that with a wave of his hand. 'No, I mean something *real*, something *professional* – that's what I've been wanting to do for you.'

'Well . . .'

'I'll feel really good doing it. 'Cause I'll know, you see, I'll know that Mr P.'d be grateful.'

'I'm sure he would have been. But it's not going to be too difficult . . . ?'

'Mrs P.,' he reassured her, 'it'll be a doddle. It's only what I do for a living, isn't it?'

'Well, yes, but—'

'No buts. Come on, let's sort out the fine tuning. Now you'll want to be off tomorrow, won't you?'

'In an ideal world, yes. But that's pretty tight for you, isn't it? I mean, if it can't be done in time, of course I'll understand.'

'No problem at all, Mrs P. Leave it with me. My end of the business can be done by lunchtime tomorrow, no sweat.'

'But goodness knows what the chances of getting a flight are. I don't really feel very inclined to ask Ginnie.'

'Don't you dare. No way. Suspicious cow, that one. And she's in far too thick with Karaskakis. No, less she knows about this, the better.'

'Well, who else do we ask?'

Larry Lambeth gave a complacent smile, put down his glass of Greek brandy, and rose from the table. 'This, Mrs P., is clearly a job for HRH.'

He turned on his heel and walked quickly into the villa, leaving Mrs Pargeter to conjecture which Royal Highness might be most likely to help with her investigation.

But she felt content. Things were moving. Sergeant Karaskakis' panic had reinforced her conviction that Joyce had been murdered. Whether the policeman himself had killed her, or was only involved in the cover-up of the killing, she could not yet be sure. But she felt completely confident that she would find out the truth.

So she looked out through the night sky to Albania, sipped her retsina, and waited for Larry Lambeth to return.

He was only gone five minutes, and came back in high good humour. Rubbing his hands together with satisfaction, he sat down and topped up his tall brandy glass.

'All sorted, Mrs P., all sorted. It's on for late tomorrow afternoon. Get confirmation of the exact details in the morning. HRH was delighted to be of service.'

'I'm sorry I have to ask,' Mrs Pargeter apologised, 'but who is HRH?'

'Oh, I thought you knew. It's Hamish Ramon Henriques. Surely I mentioned him to you?'

'Well, yes, you did, but by his full name, not just the initials. You said you did a lot of work for him.'

'Sure. And he worked a lot with Mr P. That's why he was so delighted to hear from me, even at this time of night. When he heard the job was for you, he was over the moon. Fact is, he told me Mr P. had given him strict instructions to sort things out for you if ever you needed any help. You meant a lot to your husband, you know. He really looked after you, didn't he, Mrs P.?'

'Yes. Yes, he did,' said Mrs Pargeter quietly.

'Still does, and all.'

'Yes.'

'Anyway, now HRH has taken it in hand, you got no worries. He is quite simply the best in the business.'

'Yes,' said Mrs Pargeter. 'Good.' But she had to ask, 'I'm sorry – the best *what* in the business?'

'Well, he's—' But Larry Lambeth stopped himself and said mischievously, 'You'll find out soon enough. He's going to meet you at the airport himself.'

'Oh, really?'

'Unheard of, that. Hardly ever stirs from the office, old HRH. In fact, I can't think of another case I've ever heard of when he's gone and met the client himself.'

'Oh?'

'So I hope you're suitably honoured.'

'Oh. Yes. I'll say,' said Mrs Pargeter, suitably honoured but totally mystified.

Larry Lambeth spread his hands out on the table in a businesslike fashion. 'Right. Better sort out exactly what the running order's going to be for tomorrow . . .'

They were in his car on the track down to Agios Nikitas when he suddenly had another thought. 'Ooh, Mrs P., nearly forgot. Your friend's ouzo bottle . . .'

'Oh yes. Did you check out what was in it?'

'Sure.'

'And . . . ?'

'A very dilute solution of sodium carbonate.'

'Oh.' It was a long, long time since Mrs Pargeter had done any chemistry. 'Should that mean anything to me?'

'Well, it's quite a common laboratory chemical.'

'Poisonous?'

'Wouldn't taste very nice, but you'd be hard put to kill yourself with it.'

'What about killing someone else?'

'No way. There are a lot of easier ways of getting rid of people.'

'Hm. So what is it used for?'

'Any number of things. It's used in glass-making . . .'

'Oh thanks. So far as I know, Joyce didn't come out here to make glass.'

'It's an ingredient in bath salts.'

'But is she likely to have brought it out in that form to use as bath salts?'

'Extremely unlikely. Particularly as almost all the villas out here have got showers rather than baths, anyway.' He bit his lip pensively. 'Sodium carbonate's used in various household cleaners. Not that different from washing soda, in some ways.'

'I'm sure she wouldn't have brought it out here as a cleaner, Larry. She'd got a travel-pack of detergent in her case, anyway.'

'Hm. Well . . . sodium carbonate's also used in various water-softening processes . . .'

'I suppose it's possible Joyce was worried about the effect of hard water on her skin or—'

But Larry Lambeth dismissed that idea. 'Nah. You'd never bring out neat sodium carbonate for that. If you was really worried about it, you'd be much more likely to use some of the proprietary water-softening tablets.'

'Hm.' Mrs. Pargeter was thoughtful. 'Anything else it's used for?'

'Well,' said Larry Lambeth, unable to suppress a giggle in his voice, 'sodium carbonate is actually used in the process of extracting tungsten from wulframite.'

'Is it?' said Mrs Pargeter wryly. 'Well, thank you very much. Amazing I've got this far into my life without knowing that, isn't it, Larry?'

23

Mrs Pargeter spent a quiet morning, pottering round Agios Nikitas. She told Maria at breakfast that she was going on a trip to see a little more of the island. A hire-car was coming to pick her up after lunch to take her to Corfu Town for some shopping. She would stay in a hotel there, and the next day have a hire-car to take her to see the natural beauties of Paleokastritsa on the west coast. Another night in the hotel in Corfu Town, then back to Agios Nikitas.

Oh, Maria said in dismay, Mrs Pargeter should have booked the hire-car through the Hotel Nausica. The rates would have been much cheaper than through Spiro. He always put a big mark-up on everything.

Mrs. Pargeter said, oh how silly of her, she would remember that another time. Then she asked if Maria would mind having her photograph taken in front of the hotel. Even better, would her father and mother and the rest of the family come out and have their photographs taken in front of the hotel? Mrs Pargeter knew she wasn't leaving yet, but she really did want photographs of them all as souvenirs, and it was the kind of thing she might easily forget.

All the family members were delighted to have their photographs taken.

Then, pausing only to drop by the minimarket and buy a large white cotton hat and large pair of sunglasses (both of which she kept hidden in a carrier-bag), Mrs Pargeter went across to have a drink at Spiro's. It was early for retsina, so she asked Yianni for a Sprite.

Linda from South Woodham Ferrers was at the taverna, trying unsuccessfully to get Craig, who had had a stomach upset the night before, to eat some yoghurt. Keith was working out on his calculator how much more the anti-diarrhoea medicine cost on Corfu than it did in South Woodham Ferrers. From time to time he wondered, out loud, how things were going back at the office.

The Secretary with Short Bleached Hair and the Secretary with Long Bleached Hair were sulking in the shade of Spiro's awning, sipping Nescafé. They had been to a discotheque in Ipsos the night before, where they had both fancied the same plasterer from Bradford. He had flirted and danced with each sufficiently to start them quarrelling, and then compounded that felony by going off at the end of the evening with a hairdresser from Luton who – adding insult to injury – had a perfect tan.

The two secretaries' sunburn had now reached a threshold of unsightliness and pain which had forced them to spend a day in the shade, but the previous night's row still festered and they kept snapping at each other.

At a table near the taverna door sat Spiro, Georgio and Sergeant Karaskakis, together, surprisingly, with Theodosia, who had been granted a rare moment's respite from the kitchen. Georgio was keeping a distant eye on Ginnie, who sat at a nearby table, patiently listening to more gripes from Mr and Mrs Safari Suit. The couple were wearing different clothes that day. Slightly greener in colour. Still safari suits, of course.

Spiro wandered over amiably to chat to Mrs Pargeter. He hoped she was getting over the dreadful shock of her friend's death. It was terrible that anyone should do such a thing to themselves, wasn't it?

Oh yes, Mrs Pargeter agreed, terrible.

Still, Spiro continued reassuringly, soon everything would be sorted out. The dead woman's daughter had arrived to complete the formalities, did Mrs Pargeter know that?

Yes, yes, she said, she had met Conchita the night before.

How terrible, said Spiro, for a young girl to have her mother do such a thing to herself, wasn't it?

Oh yes, Mrs Pargeter agreed, terrible.

Having fielded these commiserations, she then outlined to Spiro the plans for her trip to see a little more of the island.

Oh, he said in dismay, Mrs Pargeter should have booked the hire-car through Spiro. The rates would have been much cheaper than through the Hotel Nausica. They always put a big mark-up on everything.

Mrs Pargeter said, oh how silly of her, she would remember that another time. Then she asked if Spiro would mind having his photograph taken in front of the taverna. Even better, would Yianni and Theodosia and Georgio mind having their photographs taken in front of the taverna? Mrs Pargeter knew she wasn't leaving yet, but she really did want photographs of all of them as souvenirs, and it was the kind of thing she might easily forget.

Spiro and his staff were delighted to have their photographs taken.

The first one Mrs Pargeter took of Spiro she wasn't satisfied with, because her hand slipped just as she was pressing the button, but he was very happy to pose again. So were all of them, except for Theodosia, who seemed to be shy of the camera. But her brother snapped a command at her in Greek and, though still clearly unwilling, she submitted to being photographed.

Mrs Pargeter even asked Sergeant Karaskakis if she could take a snap of him. He was positively delighted to be so honoured, and could not keep a leer of triumph out of his face as the shutter clicked.

Back at the Hotel Nausica, Mrs Pargeter picked up from Reception the expected padded envelope, which had been delivered by motorcycle courier, and sat down to eat an early lunch. In the course of this, a second padded envelope was delivered for her. After lunch she went upstairs to pack her flightbag for her trip 'to see a little more of the island'.

She was waiting outside the Hotel Nausica in a rather bulky cotton print dress and straw hat when, on the dot of two o'clock, the hire-car arrived. (It had been arranged by Larry Lambeth from a firm in Corfu Town.)

The driver was uncommunicative, which suited Mrs Pargeter well, but she did not risk opening either of the envelopes while she was in his car. Though he was from a different part of the island, she didn't rule out the possibility of information homing straight back to Agios Nikitas.

The journey along the switchback coast road was dusty, but not unpleasant. As instructed, the driver deposited her in Corfu Town at the north end of the Esplanade. He asked for no money; Larry Lambeth had sorted that out.

There was no play that afternoon on Corfu's famous but eternally incongruous cricket pitch. The sun was baking, and Mrs Pargeter felt drawn towards the shade of the Liston, a Parisian-style colonnade of street cafés, where tourists lounged lethargically.

But her instructions did not include stopping for a cold drink, so she moved sedately through the sunlight towards the Palace of St Michael and St George.

A car slid alongside her. The door opened. She got in the back.

'Well done,' said Larry Lambeth.

Safely inside the car, she changed her straw hat for the new white cotton one and put on the new sunglasses. Then she unbuttoned the bright dress and slipped it off to reveal a sober, anonymous beige one beneath.

'Quite a relief to have that off,' she sighed. 'Hot weather for two dresses.'

Larry Lambeth chuckled.

Mrs Pargeter finally turned her attention to the two padded envelopes. The first one contained a first class airline ticket. Olympic Airways. Five o'clock scheduled flight for that afternoon. Corfu to London Heathrow. Clipped to the ticket was a 'With Compliments' slip headed 'HRH Travel'.

She turned her attention to the second envelope. 'So who am I, Larry?' she asked.

'You have a look, Mrs P.'

It was a perfect job. A British passport in the name of 'Mrs Joan Frimley Wainwright', a 'Housewife' whose place of birth had been 'Norwich'. The date of birth tallied for Mrs Pargeter, as did the height. And the photograph looked astonishingly like the passport's new holder.

'Where did you get it from, Larry?'

He shrugged. 'Saw her on the beach at Kalami this morning. Right size, right age. Mind you, she was a real old biddy, hadn't got your style at all, Mrs P.'

Mrs Pargeter's compassion was aroused. 'But won't she be terribly upset to lose her passport?'

'Happens all the time,' said Larry callously. 'She'll survive.'

Mrs Pargeter gave another look to what really did seem to be a picture of herself. 'How on earth did you fix the photograph, Larry? And how on earth did you do it so quickly?'

He grinned proudly. 'Fact is, we all have our professional secrets, don't we, Mrs P.?'

Mrs Pargeter looked around anxiously at Corfu Airport, but there was no sign of the Customs officer who looked so like Sergeant Karaskakis.

There were no problems about checking in luggage, as she only had her flightbag.

There were no problems at Passport Control.

There were no problems with the flight. It left on time.

In fact, there were no problems at all.

But, in spite of that, as she sat in her first class seat, serviced by solicitous stewardesses, Mrs Pargeter was ill at ease.

The passport for Mrs Joan Frimley Wainwright in her handbag felt as if it was on fire. Soon the flames would burst out and everyone would have their attention drawn to the forgery.

Mrs Pargeter felt dreadful.

It was the first time in her life, you see, that she had ever broken the law.

24

It was a huge relief to be safely through Passport Control at Heathrow.

And an even huger relief to have someone there to meet her.

'Good afternoon, Mrs Pargeter. I am Hamish Ramon Henriques.'

He took her hand and bowed down to kiss it. He was in his sixties, very tall and very British in dress. In spite of the mild June weather, he wore one of those three-piece tweed suits that look as if they have been marinated in family history. He had brown shoes built like rowing-boats and some sort of regimental tie. His accent epitomised the impeccable vagueness of the British upper classes.

But his face contradicted all these impressions. The skin was coffee with a dash of milk, and eyes like black olives crowded either side of the fine prow of his nose.

All his features seemed lengthened, pulled down, as in a painting by El Greco. Centrally-parted white hair swept down over his ears and a long carefully-nurtured white moustache drooped over his full lips. He looked like an illustration of Don Quixote.

But he was no mere tilter at windmills. With exemplary efficiency, he whisked Mrs Pargeter through the terminal crowds and out to a limousine which waited, unmolested by traffic authorities, in the Strictly-No-Parking area directly outside the exit. The chauffeur needed no instructions but swept effortlessly through the traffic on to the M4.

'I have booked you into the Savoy,' said Hamish Ramon Henriques. 'I gather you are always happy to stay there.'

'Yes. That'll be very nice indeed, thank you.'

'I have spoken to Truffler Mason. He will meet you in the bar at six o'clock.'

'Oh, that is kind. Let's hope he has got something to report.'

'In my experience, he is always very reliable. I have never known Truffler Mason not to come up with information in an investigation.'

'Well, that's comforting. You've worked with him a lot, have you?'

Hamish Ramon Henriques made an expansive gesture. 'My dear Mrs Pargeter, I have worked with everyone. Particularly of course with your late husband.' He looked soulful. 'The business lost a great deal when he died, you know.'

'Yes,' Mrs Pargeter agreed pensively.

'No, he was a man with standards. Nowadays some of the people I have to work for . . .' – Hamish Ramon Henriques gave a very Latin shrug – 'they are utterly immoral. They have no sense of right and wrong.'

Mrs Pargeter fervently endorsed this opinion. 'I know, it's dreadful, isn't it?'

'With your late husband, one always knew where one stood. His operations were always efficient and so it was a pleasure to contribute one's own efficiency to them.'

'And, er,' Mrs Pargeter asked cautiously, 'you have always been involved in the transport side of things, have you?'

'Yes. I started in a very modest way back in the Fifties. Procuring and renting out getaway cars.'

'Oh yes?'

'But then the business expanded into other areas of transport. Obviously a lot of run-of-the-mill travel arrangements to predictable destinations . . . the Costa del Sol, certain South American countries . . . for people who needed to be out of England for a while. In fact, I once organised a trip of that kind for you and your late husband.'

'Did you?'

'Yes. To Crete. Do you remember it?'

'Certainly. We had a wonderful time. I didn't know you arranged that.'

Hamish Ramon Henriques nodded with diffident pride. 'It was my privilege. Quite tricky at the time, actually. They were looking out for him at the airports.'

'Really?' It did explain something, though. 'Is that why he went on the plane dressed as a bishop?'

'Yes. The late Mr Pargeter was the Bishop of Tristan da Cunha, travelling to an Interdenominational Ecumenical Conference in Heraklion.'

'Good heavens.'

'That's what it said on the passport. Didn't you see it?'

Mrs Pargeter smiled apologetically. 'No, he always looked after the passports. By the way,' she added, 'who did I go as?'

Hamish Ramon Henriques looked bewildered. 'Well, obviously – the wife of the Bishop of Tristan da Cunha. Who did you think you would have gone as?'

She giggled. 'I don't know. Thought I might have been an actress.'

Hamish Ramon Henriques didn't see the joke. 'No, no, that wouldn't have done at all. Very important in my area of the travel business that one avoids immorality. It doesn't do to draw attention to oneself.'

'No, no, of course not,' said Mrs Pargeter, suitably chastened. 'And the company's still going well, is it?'

'I'll say. Everyone's travelling more these days, so of course there's a knock-on effect at my end of the business.'

'Good.'

'No, all going extremely well. I keep having to take on more staff. And of course I can charge rather more than the average travel agent for . . . you know, those little extras.'

'Little extras like what?'

He grinned. 'Confidentiality . . . secrecy . . . bodyguards . . . not going to the police, that kind of thing.'

'Oh yes, of course. Incidentally, while we're on the subject, do let me know what I owe you. I'd hate for you to—'

He raised his hands in horror. She had uttered blasphemy. 'Mrs Pargeter, I would not dream of charging you anything. After all your late husband did for me in the early years of my business, all the work he put my way . . . I am almost insulted that you even mention it.'

'Oh, I'm so sorry'

'Very well. We say no more about it.'

'If you insist.'

'I do. Suffice it to say that, without your late husband's support and faith, my company would certainly not have the pre-eminent position and reputation that it now enjoys.'

'Oh, I see. Hm. Well . . . ' Mrs Pargeter felt that a change of subject would be appropriate, and prompted,

'I dare say you've done some pretty big jobs in your time . . . ?'

Hamish Ramon Henriques was more than happy to recount his triumphs. 'I'll say. Tricky one we did a few years back was that racehorse. You remember hearing about a horse called . . . Shergar?'

'Oh yes.'

'Well, that did present problems. I mean, easy enough to arrange transport for horses here – not so easy to fly them out to the southern hemisphere.'

'I'm sure it isn't. Is he still out there?'

'I'll say. Oh yes, Shergar's going to confuse the bloodlines of international racing for a good few years yet.'

'I suppose I shouldn't ask which part of the southern hemisphere it was, should I?'

'Well, of course I'd tell you, but—'

'No, shouldn't have even raised the question.' Mrs Pargeter remembered the late Mr Pargeter's views. 'Some things better I don't know.'

'Right.'

'So, Mr Henriques—'

'Please call me HRH. Everyone does.'

'Right. So, HRH, would you say that Shergar was the biggest job you've ever done?'

'Maybe. Mind you . . . ' – he lowered his voice confidentially – 'the one I'm proudest of is Lord Lucan.'

'Oh really,' said Mrs Pargeter. 'You made his travel arrangements, did you?'

Hamish Ramon Henriques nodded modestly.

'Well, HRH, I don't think I'll ask about his destination either.'

'I'd tell you of course if you wanted to know, but . . . perhaps better not.'

'Right.'

'He's still out there, actually.'

'Oh?'

'Haven't seen him for a few years, but, er . . . I still get Christmas cards.'

'Ah.'

The carphone rang and the chauffeur answered it. 'Crooks' Tours.'

Hamish Ramon Henriques burst into a torrent of Spanish expletives. 'Don't you dare ever say that again!' he roared at the chauffeur.

'Sorry. Wasn't thinking. It's for you, Mr Henriques.'

His face still red with fury, Hamish Ramon Henriques picked up the extension.

'Do please tell me,' he said, as the car bowled effortlessly along the Westway into London, 'if there is any other service you require. Anything you need doing, my staff and I are at your disposal round the clock.'

'Thank you.'

'Is there anything?'

'No, I don't think . . . Ooh yes, I wonder – would it be possible to get some photographs developed rather quickly?'

'Of course. Give the film to me and I will see that the prints are delivered to the Savoy within the hour.'

He took the film and handed her a printed card. 'If there's anything else you require, ring this number. Or do feel welcome to call in at our offices in Berkeley Square.'

'Thank you so much. There was one thing I wanted to ask you, HRH . . .'

'Ask away.'

'Have you ever heard of someone called Chris Dover . . . ?'

'Hm. Bloke who used to deal in arms back in the early Sixties – that the one?'

'Yes.'

'Came from South America somewhere, didn't he?'

'Uruguay.'

'That's right.'

'Well, I just wondered if you'd ever had any dealings with him. You know, because he must have had a lot of travel arrangements, given his line of work. And of course he could have spoken Spanish to you, couldn't he?'

'Yes. But no, I never did do anything for him. And that's strange, really, because at that stage I was the only person in London in my line of business. There are a lot more now – I mean, HRH is still far and away the best – but there is more competition these days.'

'So you never even met Chris Dover?'

'No. And I know he was aware of what I did, because I heard from people who'd recommended my services to him. But he never made contact. And in fact, now I come to remember it, there were two or three occasions – you know, social functions – which we were both invited to, and each time he just didn't turn up.'

'Coincidence.'

'Mmm,' said Hamish Ramon Henriques ruminatively. 'More than coincidence I remember thinking at the time.'

'Oh?'

'Yes. Almost as if Chris Dover was deliberately trying to avoid me.'

25

Hamish Ramon Henriques had organised a range of clothes from her home wardrobe to be in Mrs Pargeter's room in the Savoy and, after a bath, she selected a coral-coloured silk suit for her meeting with Truffler Mason.

The late Mr Pargeter had always encouraged his wife to wear bright colours. 'No point in trying to hide yourself, my dear,' he had frequently said, 'when there's such a delicious amount of you to hide.'

She cut a handsome figure in the Savoy bar. Truffler Mason looked less exotic. He wore his customary camouflage of nondescript sports jacket and brown trousers. His long, horse-like face looked even more gloomy than usual.

'Virtually nothing to report, Mrs Pargeter,' he apologised. 'I've spent most of the day on the phone to contacts in Uruguay and still haven't got any positive identification or details about Chris Dover's life before he came to England.'

'It was a long time ago.'

'Yes. What's more, he seems to have slipped out of the country secretly, so there probably wouldn't be any records.'

'And you didn't find anything from his time in Uruguay back in the house?'

Truffler didn't ask how she knew he'd searched the Dover family home. That was one of the things he liked about working for Mrs Pargeter. So little explanation was necessary. She understood his methods and just let him get on with it.

'No. He seems to have covered his tracks very effectively. I went through everything. There was some kid's stuff, but it was all Sindy Dolls and what have you – clearly the daughter's. I only found one thing that might have belonged to Chris when he was younger.'

'What was that?'

'A chemistry set. Kid's chemistry set.'

'Oh. Where had it been manufactured?' Mrs Pargeter asked hopefully.

'In England,' Truffler Mason replied, immediately dashing her hopes of a Uruguayan connection.

‘Ah.’ Another thought came to her. ‘Was there any sodium carbonate in the set?’

‘Didn’t notice. I’d have to check again.’

‘It’s probably not important. What was the chemistry set like?’

‘Fairly small set-up. A few test-tubes, a few little pots of chemicals. Manufactured in England, as I say. Done a bit of research and it seems it would have been available in toyshops here round the late Fifties.’

‘Just about the time Chris came over here. So he probably bought it soon after he arrived . . .’

‘Perhaps.’

‘Maybe, for someone new to the country, that was the easiest way he could find of obtaining chemicals he needed.’

‘Possible.’

‘But I wonder what he needed them for . . . ? Hm, we have no means of knowing. Too many things in this case at the moment that we have no means of knowing.’ She slumped back into her chair, dissatisfied, and sipped her vodka martini. ‘There’s something here in England which explains why Joyce was murdered.’

‘What makes you so sure of that?’

Mrs Pargeter told Truffler about her encounter with Sergeant Karaskakis. ‘It was the speed with which he changed tack when I said I would go back to England to investigate. Up until then he’d been trying to persuade me to leave. The sooner I got out of Corfu and out of his hair, the better. But the moment I said – I was only bluffing, but I said I could produce evidence from England that Joyce had been murdered – and the moment I said it, suddenly he was desperate to keep me on the island until the investigation was over. Which must mean that I had somehow stumbled on the truth. There actually *is* proof of the murder – or proof of the motive for the murder – over here. If only I knew what I was looking for.’

Truffler gave his long chin a contemplative stroke. 'The night Joyce Dover was murdered . . .'

'Mm?'

'You said that her suitcases had been searched . . .'

'Yes. So had mine.'

'And what do you think whoever did it was looking for?'

'Well, I'd assumed it was the ouzo bottle, which by chance was in my flightbag down at Spiro's all the time.'

'Suppose they were looking for something else, too?'

'I don't know. There wasn't anything else you noticed that was missing?'

'No. Mind you, I'd assumed it was the ouzo bottle they were after, so I didn't look very hard.'

Truffler looked, if possible, more depressed than ever as he asked, 'Joyce didn't mention any letter, did she?'

'Letter?'

'Letter from her husband. Letter that she was to be given after his death.'

'No, I don't think . . .' Suddenly Mrs Pargeter recalled Joyce's words. 'She did say something about Chris still trying to control her from beyond the grave and . . . Yes, yes, now I come to think of it, she did mention a letter.'

'But you didn't see it? She didn't show it to you?'

'No.'

'Just suppose for a moment,' said Truffler slowly, 'that that letter was the reason why she went to Corfu in the first place . . . ?'

'You mean that she was following Chris's instructions? That it wasn't just a random decision to go to Greece? She deliberately chose Agios Nikitas?'

'Mm. It'd make more sense of the murder. At least it would mean she had some connection with someone out there.'

'Yes.'

'You say she didn't show you the letter. And you didn't see a sign of any such letter when you went through her luggage after you'd found her body?'

'No.'

'Maybe that was what the murderer was searching for . . . ? Maybe the murderer found the letter and took it . . . ?'

'We're assuming here that Joyce had got it with her, aren't we?'

'Oh, I think that's a reasonable assumption, Mrs Pargeter. I mean, if you were to receive a letter giving you detailed instructions to go somewhere you'd never been before, you'd take it with you when you went there, wouldn't you? To check details, that kind of thing.'

'Yes, all right, I agree. I probably would. But there's another, bigger assumption we're making, and I'm not so convinced that that one is reasonable.'

'What assumption?'

'The assumption that such a letter existed in the first place.'

'It existed all right,' said Truffler with calm assurance.

'How do you know?'

'Because I've spoken to the solicitor who gave it to Mrs Dover.'

'Was that the one you mentioned to me on the phone? Double-barrelled name . . . ?'

'Fisher-Metcalf, that's right. Used to be Chris Dover's solicitor. I went to see him yesterday, and I've fixed an appointment for you to go and see him at ten o'clock tomorrow morning.'

'But no solicitor worth his salt is going to discuss the affairs of one of his clients, even if that client is dead – I mean, unless it's the police or someone official making the enquiries.'

'Mrs Pargeter, I wouldn't be so sure that Mr Fisher-Metcalf *is* worth his salt. I'm confident that he can be persuaded to talk.'

'You mean you've got something on him, Truffler?'

The satisfaction on the private detective's face was so positive that he almost looked cheerful.

'Yes, Mrs Pargeter, I've got something on him.'

26

The office was in Hackney and so drab that it looked like something out of a Fifties British B-feature. The adenoidal girl who let Mrs Pargeter into her anteroom would not have looked out of place in the same movie. Lank, dull hair, droopy cardigan, shapeless kilt in some tartan Mrs Pargeter did not recognise. Certainly not an obvious one like the Black Watch or Hunting Stuart. Moping Mactavish, perhaps?

'If you'd just wait a moment,' said the girl, as if through a nasal drip, 'I'll tell Mr Fisher-Metcalf you're here.'

Mrs Pargeter sat on a cracked mock-leather chair and gazed on a dispiriting vista of faded green box-files. Whatever inroads the new technology might have made elsewhere, it hadn't penetrated this little corner of post-war Britain. The telephone on the desk was a black Bakelite one, and the old manual typewriter, stuffed with a sheaf of paper and carbons, looked like a close relative of an eighteenth-century threshing machine. Only the dangling overhead light with its parchment shade confirmed that the place even had electricity laid on.

Over everything lay a thick blurring of dust. The room smelled of dust. And of something else, less pleasant, as though a cracked drain had been seeping quietly into the foundations for a couple of centuries.

The girl drooped back into the room with an apologetic sniff. 'If you'd like to come through . . .'

Mrs Pargeter, glad that the purple and yellow flowers of her silk dress were bringing a splash of colour into this murk of greens and beiges, went through into Mr Fisher-Metcalf's office.

Its owner would easily have qualified for a part in the same film as his secretary. Shiny pin-striped suit, white shirt, a tie patterned with dots so tiny that the effect was uniform black. His bald head was inadequately disguised with a meagre combing of salt-and-pepper hair. His face drooped with defeat, apology and a degree of guilt.

'Good morning,' he said. 'Mrs Pargeter, isn't it? Won't you take a seat?' The anaemic secretary still lingered in the doorway. 'Perhaps you'd like a cup of coffee . . . ?'

The smell of the anteroom had put Mrs Pargeter off the idea of anything prepared out there, so she refused the offer. The secretary vanished with a farewell sniff.

'Now, Mrs Pargeter, what can I do for you?'

The apology in his tone expressed a whole lifetime of failure. Clearly Mr Fisher-Metcalf had never quite been up to any of the challenges life had offered him. He had just scraped through exams at school, then just scraped through his legal exams, fortunate to be entering a self-perpetuating profession.

Though Mrs Pargeter knew some excellent solicitors – indeed, she owed the fact that she and the late Mr Pargeter had not been prevented from spending more of their married life together to the good offices of the famous Arnold Justiman – she did not have a very high opinion of the profession. She knew it to be one in which talent was not of paramount importance. The British legal system – created, of course, by solicitors – guarantees undemanding and lucrative employment for life to anyone who can be crammed up to qualify.

So she didn't really think she was going to have too much trouble dealing with Mr Fisher-Metcalf.

'I want to talk about your late client, Mr Chris Dover.'

A cloud of professional affront crossed the solicitor's face. 'I'm afraid it is not proper for me to discuss the affairs of my clients, whether living or dead.'

'Ah,' said Mrs Pargeter. No point in delaying the offensive. Time was of the essence to her investigation. 'And would that still be the case if I were to tell you that I know all about Harry Thackeray?'

'I don't know what you're talking about.' It was bluster. He was already defeated, as easily pushed over as a cardboard cutout.

'What I'm talking about is the case four years back when Harry Thackeray was accused of organising a protection racket in Canning Town. I know you were involved.'

'Of course I was involved. I was acting for Mr Thackeray in my professional capacity.'

'I was talking about what you did in a less professional capacity.'

'Oh?'

'Funny what happened there, wasn't it? Looked like the prosecution had a cast-iron case against Harry Thackeray. All those publicans, restaurant owners, shopkeepers, all prepared to testify that they had been menaced, threatened, beaten up in some cases – do you remember that poor Bengali with the two broken arms? And then, suddenly, night before the case, they all spontaneously decided that their recollections were a bit hazy and that they didn't want to testify, after all.'

'People have the right to change their minds.'

'Oh, sure. Yes. One of the greatest human rights, that. Funny they should all change their minds at the same time, though, wasn't it?'

'Coincidences do happen.'

'Yes,' Mrs Pargeter agreed. 'Like the coincidence that

all of those witnesses had visits the day before the case from rather big men with baseball bats – men who, it seems, didn't even appear to know the rules of baseball.'

He still clung on to the last shreds of his bluff. 'I don't know why you're telling me all this, Mrs Pargeter.'

'I'm just reminding you that you organised those visits by the men with baseball bats.'

'You don't have any proof of that.'

Unhurried, Mrs Pargeter opened her handbag and pulled out some papers. She put them on Mr Fisher-Metcalf's desk. 'These are the names and addresses of the men who made the visits, and at the bottom you'll find signed statements by two of them as to whose orders they were obeying. These are only photocopies, obviously.'

'Oh.' The cardboard cutout was now flat and unresisting on the floor.

'"Pincer" Cartwright and "Dumptruck" Donnellan.' Mrs Pargeter smiled sweetly. 'What quaint names.'

Good old Truffler, she thought. Never fails to come up with the goods.

The solicitor moistened his lips with a wormlike tongue. 'Are you from the police?'

Mrs Pargeter let out a peal of laughter. 'Good heavens, no. Far from it. Like any normal, law-abiding citizen, I have always tried to have as little to do with the police as possible. No, as I said, all I want to do is get some information about the late Chris Dover. If I get that information, I certainly wouldn't feel any need to go near the police.'

'Ah. Good. Well, Mrs Pargeter, I'm sure I would be able to reconsider my decision about discussing Mr Dover's affairs . . . given the, er, rather unusual circumstances . . .'

'Oh, good.'

'What, er, information do you require?'

'Well, let's start with how long you'd known Chris Dover.'

'A long time. I've acted for him ever since I qualified.'

'And when was that?'

'The early Sixties.'

'Ah. Before he started his own company.'

'Yes.'

'In fact, while his activities were still criminal.'

He was once again all professional formality. 'Mrs Pargeter, that is not a word whose use I can condone in relation to my clients.'

'What word do you prefer then? Illegal? Illicit? Felonious? Crooked?' Mrs Pargeter grinned. 'Do stop me when you hear one whose use you can condone.'

Mr Fisher-Metcalf cleared his throat awkwardly. 'Well, perhaps one could say that Chris Dover was then at a stage when he was still . . . er, finding his way in life.'

'All right. Let's say that. We both know what we mean, after all, don't we?' She paused as a new idea struck her. 'Ooh, I've just had a thought . . . Did Chris Dover pay to put you through law school?'

The solicitor shifted uncomfortably and Mrs Pargeter knew that she had again stumbled on the truth. The late Mr Pargeter had done the same thing – that's what had made her think of it.

In spite of the demands of his many and varied activities, her husband had always found time for charity. He had put two young men and one young woman through law school and philanthropically continued to support them by keeping them continuously in work from the moment they had qualified as solicitors. It was clear that Chris Dover had also seen the two-way benefits to be achieved by training his own tame lawyer.

'Yes, I understand,' said Mrs Pargeter. 'You were with him all the way. You knew all about his business dealings, didn't you?'

'I can assure you,' he began, a little of his bluster reasserting itself, 'that from the time of Mr Dover's setting up his company in 1963, nothing occurred that would not withstand the most detailed scrutiny by any kind of investigating authority you care to mention.'

'No. I'm sure. Though the same couldn't be said of his activities before 1963.'

A sly look came into Mr Fisher-Metcalf's eyes. 'Of that period, I'm afraid, there are no records that could be investigated.'

'No, there wouldn't be, would there? Still, you can talk to me about that period, can't you?'

'I'm not sure that it would be proper for—'

Mrs Pargeter pointed to the papers on his desk. 'Would it be more "proper" for the police to read what "Pincer" Cartwright and "Dumptruck" Donnellan had to say about the Harry Thackeray case?'

He knew she held all the cards. 'What do you want to know?'

'I want to know about Chris Dover's early life.'

'He was brought up in Uruguay.'

'I know that. I want more detail.'

Mr Fisher-Metcalf spread his hands apologetically. 'I'm afraid I don't have any more detail. He never talked about it.'

'Never?'

'Not a single word.'

Mrs Pargeter reckoned that the solicitor was telling the truth. Conchita had said the same thing, after all.

'You said that all records of his early years in London have been destroyed?'

Even with his back against the wall, the solicitor did not abandon his professional tendency towards nit-picking. 'I said in fact that there are no records that could be investigated.'

'Is there a difference?'

'Oh yes,' he replied with the satisfaction of the nit-picker rewarded. 'Oh yes.'

'So you mean that there were records?'

'For those who knew where to look for them, yes.'

Mrs Pargeter had had enough of this coyness. 'You're saying you have got records of Chris Dover's gun-running then?'

He winced at this indecorously specific mention of the crime. 'Well . . . Yes, certain details were noted down, but . . . er, not in a way that many people would be able to understand them.'

'In shorthand, you mean?'

'Not shorthand, no.'

Mrs Pargeter picked up the papers on his desk and reasserted her dominance. 'Listen, you tell me exactly what you mean or this lot goes straight to the police!'

He looked like an Islamic Fundamentalist who had just been made to swallow a large Scotch. 'Oh, very well.'

'So how did Chris Dover keep these records?'

'If there was ever something that he needed to send me, some information that he wanted kept secret, he would hide it on a totally innocuous document.'

'Hide it? In code?'

'Not code, no. What he would do was send me a letter about something totally mundane, an acknowledgement of a letter from me, that kind of thing . . . but the important information would be written on the back.'

Suddenly a whole sequence of logic clicked into place in Mrs Pargeter's mind. 'In invisible ink?' she breathed softly.

'Effectively, yes. Chris knew a certain amount about chemistry, I think he'd experimented with it as a child. And he found out that he could write something in one chemical which was completely invisible until it was washed over with a solution of another chemical.'

Her violet blue eyes sparkled. 'Yes. Yes, of course.'

'The chemical he used for the writing was phenolphthalein,' said Mr Fisher-Metcalf, 'and the solution which had to be washed over it to bring out the information was—'

'Sodium carbonate,' said Mrs Pargeter.

27

Mr Fisher-Metcalf gaped in surprise, but Mrs Pargeter didn't give him time to respond. Her mind was moving too quickly to be delayed by pedestrian explanations.

'Listen, Chris Dover left a letter for his wife, didn't he? A letter that was to be given to her after his death?'

'Now I'm not sure that—'

'I know he did. Joyce mentioned it to me.'

'Oh.'

'By the way, did you know that Joyce was dead?'

'I had been informed, yes. It's very sad, isn't it?' he said with formality untinged by sincerity.

'What's sad?'

'That someone could be in so reduced a state, have such low self-esteem, actually to get to the point of killing themselves.'

Mrs Pargeter didn't contest this interpretation of the death. She knew she should minimise the number of people with whom she shared her suspicions. It was interesting, though, to see how quickly Sergeant Karaskakis' version of events had become the accepted one, even before it had been officially sanctioned.

'Yes, very sad,' she agreed briskly. 'Did Joyce stand to inherit a lot of money?'

'Well . . .'

Mr Fisher-Metcalf had come over all cautious and solicitorlike again, but Mrs Pargeter wasn't standing for any of that. 'Come on, what was Chris Dover worth?'

'He was an extremely wealthy man.'

'So Joyce was a very wealthy woman and would have been even wealthier after his death?' And yet, Mrs Pargeter mused, she still chose a relatively cheap package tour to Corfu as a holiday.

'Well . . .' Mr Fisher-Metcalf started to equivocate again.

'There wasn't anything funny about the will? She would have got the lot?'

'The bulk of the estate, certainly.'

'And now she's dead, it'll go to Conchita? Joyce left a will, presumably?'

'Yes, everything will all be as straightforward as it can be in a situation where both spouses die within such a short time – which is not of course completely straightforward because the legal requirements—'

Mrs Pargeter was in no mood to be delayed by this sort of stuff. 'But basically Conchita gets the lot?'

'Their daughter will inherit everything, yes.'

'Hm. Back to this letter Chris left for his wife . . .'

The solicitor looked pained. Perhaps he imagined Mrs Pargeter had forgotten raising the subject. If so, he had seriously underestimated his questioner.

'What about the letter, Mrs Pargeter?'

'Do you have a copy?'

'No. Well, that is to say, yes, I do have a copy, but I don't think you'll—'

'Could I see it please?'

'You'll be very disappointed if you—'

'Could I see it please?'

Mrs Pargeter had a knack of raising the impact of her speech without raising its volume. Her intonation on the second 'Could I see it please?' was only marginally different from that on the first, but its force was recognisably greater.

Mr Fisher-Metcalf crumbled instantly in the face of its power. He pressed an old-fashioned bell-push on his desk and the wan secretary trickled in. She was given instructions on where to find the relevant document and went out to trawl through the dusty box-files.

'Tell me,' Mrs Pargeter asked, 'to your knowledge, did Chris Dover ever have any contacts with Greece – Corfu in particular?'

The solicitor shook his head. 'Never went there, I'm sure. Never mentioned any connections either. No . . . Well, except there was one incident which I suppose . . . But no. I'm afraid I have to answer no.'

Before Mrs Pargeter had time to ask more about the one mysterious 'incident', the secretary had seeped back into the room bearing an open box-file. 'I've been right through, but I can't see any—'

'Give it to me.' Her boss stretched out an imperious hand. 'I'll find it. You go.' Before the girl was fully out of the door, he commented to Mrs Pargeter, 'So difficult to get staff with any gumption these days. Girl I had before was really efficient, but . . . she went. And the money some of the kids expect to be paid these days. It's not as if they're properly trained, either . . .'

As he wittered on about the inadequacies of modern youth, he riffled through papers in the file. Then, with satisfaction, he extracted one flimsy sheet and held it out towards the visitor. 'This is the copy, though, as I say, I don't think it'll help you much.'

It was a slightly smudged carbon, which read:

My Dearest Joyce,

I am sorry that when you receive this I will be dead. Thank you for all you have done for me. I always hoped that there would be no secrets between us, but that proved to be impossible. Still, if you really do want to know the truth, this will explain one or two things.

Your loving (but now deceased) husband,

Chris

Her eyes rose to meet a sardonic stare from Mr Fisher-Metcalf. 'Not a great deal of help, is it, Mrs Pargeter?'

'No. Surely there must have been something else with it? An enclosure of some kind?'

'There was no enclosure. No, just the one sheet of paper. And of course what you're holding there is only the copy, so that's completely useless.'

It took her a couple of seconds to catch on. 'You mean there was something written on the back of the original? In that chemical . . . whatever it was?'

Mr Fisher-Metcalf nodded graciously. 'Phenolphthalein. Yes, you're right. Chris had used his favourite method once again.'

'Did Joyce know what to do to make the writing come out? Was she expecting it?'

'No. She had no idea. I had to explain to her what I thought was likely to have happened.'

'And you were right? There was something written on the back?'

Again he inclined his head. 'There was.'

'So did you see it? Did she put on the sodium carbonate while you were present?'

'I put on the first bit myself. Mrs Dover was somewhat sceptical when I told her where I expected the message to be, so I soaked a cloth in sodium carbonate . . .' – he indicated a bottle on his shelf – 'and demonstrated it for her. Just one sweep across the paper and lettering appeared straight away. It comes up in a purplish colour, actually.'

'So did you see the whole letter?'

'No.' He sounded rather put out. 'For some reason Mrs Dover did not seem to trust my discretion.'

'I'm not surprised.'

He looked even more aggrieved, but went on, 'She said she would take it home and reveal the rest of the letter in private.'

'And presumably she didn't tell you what she found written there?'

'No, she didn't.' Once again he sounded a little resentful of this lack of confidence.

'I don't suppose, by any chance, that you remember what was on the part of the letter that you revealed here in the office . . . ?'

Mr Fisher-Metcalf smiled smugly. 'As a matter of fact, I do. My memory, you know,' he said with some pride, 'is almost photographic. A very useful faculty for a solicitor.'

Even for a bent one. But Mrs Pargeter didn't voice the thought. Instead, with a suitably impressed look, she said, 'That's remarkable. So you could actually tell me exactly what was written there, even though you only saw it once?'

The flattering approach paid off. 'Oh yes,' he replied. 'To the last letter.'

'Go on,' said Mrs Pargeter in mock-disbelief.

'The sodium carbonate only revealed part of the first word, but that ended "K-I-T-A-S". Then there was a full stop, and it went on, "If you want to find out, the explanation for everything will be found behind the old man's p—"'

' "The old man's p—"?' Mrs Pargeter echoed, disappointed.

'Yes. That was all there was. As I say, I only wiped the sodium carbonate across once.'

'Yes. Could you write that down for me, please? All the words, laid out exactly as you saw them on the page.'

While Mr Fisher-Metcalf did as he was asked, Mrs Pargeter's mind was racing. No doubt there were plenty of other words that ended 'K-I-T-A-S', but all she could think of was 'Agios Nikitas'. And, if that was what Chris Dover had written in his letter, it was the first positive proof she had of a connection between the dead man and Corfu.

What 'The old man's p—' might be she could not at that moment begin to imagine.

28

Mr Fisher-Metcalf finished writing and handed the piece of paper across to her. 'Well, Mrs Pargeter, I don't think that you can deny that I have been very helpful to you . . . answered all your questions very fully . . . but I am a busy man and I would really appreciate it if you would leave now. I'll get my secretary to—'

His finger froze above the bell-push at Mrs Pargeter's words. 'I'll go when I'm ready, thank you. When I've got all the information I require from you.'

'But—'

Her hand came to rest on the sheaf of papers Truffler Mason had given her. 'Don't let us forget,' she said with steely charm, 'who is in charge of this interview.'

Mr Fisher-Metcalf slumped back, defeated once more. 'What else do you want to know?'

'Just before your secretary came in, you said there was an "incident" which might have implied a connection between Chris Dover and Greece . . .'

'Did I? I don't recall—'

'Yes, you did, Mr Fisher-Metcalf. Come on, I haven't got time to waste. What was it?'

As ever, faced with any kind of attack, he capitulated instantly. 'Well . . . About three years ago, someone did come round to my office enquiring about Mr Dover. He wanted to find out as much as he could about how much Mr Dover was worth, about his business affairs and so on. Of course I told him it was improper for me ever to disclose any details of my clients' affairs and . . . '

'And that poor blighter didn't have anything to blackmail you with, eh?' Mrs Pargeter asked genially, her hand still gently on top of Truffler's collection of papers.

'Well, er . . .' Mr Fisher-Metcalf eased a finger round the inside of his shirt-collar. 'Well, I said I couldn't tell him anything, but he persisted . . . kept coming round, trying to pump information out of my then secretary, that kind of thing . . .'

'Did he get information?'

'Certainly not from me.'

'And from your then secretary?'

'I wouldn't have thought so. She certainly didn't mention telling him anything, and she was . . . well, she was an efficient girl . . . left the job soon afterwards, unfortunately . . . but she was nothing like that dreadful illiterate creature who's sitting out there now. I mean, there doesn't seem to be any concept of training young people these days—'

Mrs Pargeter cut short his disquisition on the failings of modern life. 'You still haven't said what the connection was between this man and Greece.'

'Ah, well, that was the point, you see. The man who made these enquiries was Greek.'

'Was he really? He didn't mention what part of Greece he came from?'

'No.'

'And you say his main interest seemed to be in Chris Dover's business affairs?'

'Yes. Well, his income, actually. He kept saying, "So Mr Dover is very rich man, yes?"'

'Did he really?'

'Yes.'

A new thought came into Mrs Pargeter's mind. She reached into her handbag. 'I've got some photographs here of a few Greek men. Could you have a look at them and tell me if any of them is the man who came to you making those enquiries?'

She opened the envelope for him. He looked at the first one. 'Well, that's most peculiar. I'd have sworn that was—'

She glanced at the picture and hastily put it to the bottom of the pack. 'Not that one. It's all overexposed. I'm sorry, I'm a dreadful photographer. I've got a much better shot of that bloke.'

The photo had been the one of Spiro she'd taken as her hand slipped. The rapid movement had almost blanked out his features completely. She found another. 'Look, there's a better shot of him. Is he familiar?'

Mr Fisher-Metcalf shook his head. He'd never seen Spiro before.

'What about this one?'

She had really been hoping for a response to the picture of Sergeant Karaskakis, but all she got was another shake of the head.

The same reaction greeted Yianni. And Maria's father and everyone else from the Hotel Nausica.

Even though they were looking for a man, she showed the picture of Theodosia, but that got the same negative response.

Without hope, Mrs Pargeter showed Mr Fisher-Metcalf the penultimate photograph.

'That's him,' the solicitor said. 'That's the one.'

The photograph was of Georgio.
'Are you sure?'
'Pretty sure.'
'Well, look, here's another one of him with—'
'Good heavens!' Mr Fisher-Metcalf was quite pale with shock.
'That's still the man, is it?'
'Oh, that's the man all right. It's the girl I'm looking at, though.'
'The girl? She's not Greek. She's English. The tour operator's rep. Ginnie.'
'Virginia, yes.'
'You know her?'
'Of course I do,' the solicitor replied testily. 'She's the one who used to be my secretary.'

29

Mrs Pargeter reckoned she had found out all she was going to find out in London, and a speedy return to Corfu was of the essence. Remembering Hamish Ramon Henriques' offer, she hailed a cab outside Mr Fisher-Metcalf's office and gave the driver the Berkeley Square address.

It was a constant source of surprise to Mrs Pargeter that businesses on the wrong side of the law conduct themselves so very much like legitimate ones. She knew this to be a naive reaction. After all, successful entrepreneurs on the two sides of the legal divide behave with astonishing similarity, and indeed there are many who spend their careers continually crossing over and back again. There was little to choose, in Mrs Pargeter's view, between the morality of the corporate raider and that of the armed raider.

And yet, in spite of this knowledge, she was still surprised by the discreet brass plate reading 'HRH Travel' on the splendid Berkeley Square portico.

The smiling, immaculately-groomed girl on Reception wore a charcoal grey uniform with a discreet 'HRH' logo in gold thread on the breast pocket. A gold badge on the other side gave her name, 'Lauren'.

'Good morning. Can I help you?'

'Yes. My name is Mrs Pargeter . . .'

'Of course. HRH said we might be expecting you.'

'Oh.'

The girl deftly pressed a button on her console. 'Sharon. Mrs Pargeter is here. Could you come and collect her? Thanks. If you'd just like to take a seat . . . ?'

Mrs Pargeter sat on the grey leather sofa and thumbed through the brochures on the low table. Except for their emphasis on Spanish and South American destinations, they were interchangeable with the literature that would have been found in any other travel agent.

'If you'd like to come this way . . .'

Sharon proved to be another smiling, immaculately-groomed girl in the same charcoal grey HRH uniform as Lauren. She led the visitor to a lift, then through a long, neat office where more smiling, immaculately-groomed girls in uniforms sat over computers and telephones. Mrs Pargeter caught snatches of their beautifully-enunciated conversations as she passed.

'. . . so could I just check this? The party will consist of yourself, two heavies and a getaway driver? Yes. What? Oh, we'll certainly reserve accommodation for a hostage as well if you think that's a possibility . . .'

'. . . yes, all the jacuzzis in the Imperial Hotel are bulletproof . . .'

'. . . so you'll arrive in Caracas on Tuesday at eleven

a.m. The plastic surgeon is booked for ten o'clock the following morning. No, don't worry, he's got a copy of the new passport photograph, so he'll ensure that's what you look like . . .'

'. . . in that part of the world there's usually no problem about getting ammunition from Room Service . . .'

Mrs Pargeter felt reassured. It was really comforting to know that one was dealing with an organisation of such efficiency.

Hamish Ramon Henriques had his office door and his arms wide open to greet her. The sunlight through the window behind him brought a sparkle to the white fringes of his Quixotic hair and moustache.

'Mrs Pargeter, what a pleasure! I trust your morning's meeting was satisfactory.'

'Yes, I managed to get quite a lot of information, thank you.'

'Excellent, excellent. And what can I do for you now?'

'Well, I don't think I'm going to get anything else, so I really would like to be back in Corfu as soon as possible. If that's not too much trouble . . .' she added modestly.

'Nothing is too much trouble for our favoured clients. And when the client is none other than the widow of the late Mr Pargeter . . .' A very Latin gesture encompassed the degree of honour and pleasure that it would be to help her out.

'Oh, thank you so much.'

'Right, let's get it organised straight away.'

He swept into the outer office with Mrs Pargeter in his wake and stopped behind the chair of the first smiling, immaculately-groomed girl in uniform.

'Karen, could you find me today's flights for Corfu? All airlines.'

'Of course, HRH.'

Buttons were punched and lines of schedules appeared on the computer screen.

'Three o'clock Olympic looks good,' said Hamish Ramon Henriques. 'Check first class availability.'

Karen punched more buttons, looked at the screen, and grimaced. 'Fully booked, I'm afraid.'

'I'd be all right in economy.' said Mrs Pargeter humbly. She might have been going against the late Mr Pargeter's principles, but knew she could cope with slumming it for three hours.

'Nonsense,' said Hamish Ramon Henriques firmly.

'Economy's full too, anyway, HRH.'

'All right, Karen. Hack into Olympic's computer.'

'Yes, HRH.' Her fingers fluttered knowledgeably over the keyboard.

'You've got today's password?'

'Of course, HRH.'

Hamish Ramon Henriques smiled at Mrs Pargeter. 'Won't take a moment.'

She was tempted to ask for an explanation of what was going on, but a lifetime spent with the late Mr Pargeter had taught her to distinguish the appropriate occasions for enquiry and ignorance. This was undoubtedly a moment for ignorance.

'Here's the first class passenger list, HRH.'

'Right.' He scanned the screen. 'Got to be someone on their own . . . Preferably foreign . . . More difficult to complain effectively if there's a language barrier . . . This one looks good – Mr Stratos Papadopoulos. Yes, do him, Karen.'

'Very good, HRH.' She moved the cursor to the end of the passenger's name and obliterated it.

'If I could just trouble you for your passport, Mrs Pargeter . . . ?'

She handed it over and Karen filled in the details of 'Mrs Joan Frimley Wainwright' on the passenger list. Then she pressed a few further controls.

'That just overrides all the other data,' Hamish Ramon

Henriques explained, 'and alters the information on the computers in Athens and Corfu.'

'But,' she couldn't help asking, 'will it really work?'

Hamish Ramon Henriques looked hurt by her lack of confidence. 'Of course, Mrs Pargeter. I pride myself on the efficiency of HRH Travel. We are doing this kind of stuff all the time, you know.'

'Yes. Yes, of course you are. I'm so sorry.'

He took her to an excellent lunch at the Connaught, where they met up with Truffler Mason, who had little new to report but was very entertaining in his habitually lugubrious way. He told them about a bigamy case he'd investigated, in which the husband was maintaining eleven wives in flats in different parts of London. 'When he got put away,' Truffler concluded, 'London Transport nearly went out of business.'

The same limousine was waiting for them outside the Connaught. Mrs Pargeter's bill at the Savoy had been settled, her belongings packed and collected. Truffler said fond farewells, passed on his regards to Larry Lambeth, assured Mrs Pargeter that if he got any more information on Chris Dover she'd know it immediately and said he was on the end of a phone any time – day or night – that she might need him.

Hamish Ramon Henriques insisted on accompanying her to Heathrow.

Inside the limousine Mrs Pargeter commented on the fact that they had a different chauffeur for this trip. A spasm of anger crossed Hamish Ramon Henriques' face. 'The other one is no longer working for me,' he hissed.

He really hadn't liked that crack about 'Crooks' Tours', had he?

At Heathrow the limousine was once again parked in the Strictly-No-Parking area and the chauffeur instructed to wait while Hamish Ramon Henriques escorted his charge into the terminal.

At the Olympic desk a large olive-skinned man was arguing noisily with one of the staff. Hamish Ramon Henriques engaged the attention of another official, who handed over Mrs Pargeter's ticket without demur.

'But this is ridiculous!' the large man was saying in heavily-accented English. 'I know full well I made the booking! Four weeks ago! It was a first class seat, confirmed by my travel agent! The name is Papadopoulos! I am an important man, you know! How you have the nerve to tell me . . .'

Mrs Pargeter moved meekly away from the desk. Well-trained as she had been by the late Mr Pargeter, she recognised yet another of those occasions when she didn't need to know all the details of what was going on.

Hamish Ramon Henriques bade her a devoted farewell, and Mrs Joan Frimley Wainwright passed unmolested through to Departures and into the first class lounge.

30

Mrs Pargeter lay back in Mr Papadopoulos's first class seat, sipping her complimentary champagne, and thought about Joyce's death.

The connections between Chris Dover and Agios Nikitas were certainly building up. A week before, Mrs Pargeter believed her friend to have selected Corfu randomly as a holiday destination, but now it was clear that Joyce had been obeying very specific instructions. If Mrs Pargeter's interpretation of the portion of the letter remembered by Mr Fisher-Metcalf was correct, then Chris Dover's directions had pointed not just to Corfu, but to Agios Nikitas itself.

Why? Why?

If only she could see that letter . . . Mrs Pargeter felt confident that Joyce had taken it with her to Corfu, and equally confident that it had been removed from the dead woman's belongings by her murderer.

She took out Mr Fisher-Metcalf's copy of what he had seen revealed by the sodium carbonate and studied it.

'—KITAS. If you want to find out, the explanation for everything will be found behind the old man's p—'

She focused on the interrupted final word for a while, but was prompted to no obvious solution. There were so many words that began with 'P' . . . Her thoughts kept turning mischievously – and unhelpfully – obscene. No, she wasn't getting anywhere on that.

She tried to process the new information she had about Georgio and Ginnie. It was the most direct connection that had yet been established between Chris Dover and Agios Nikitas. Georgio had gone to London to look into the dead man's business affairs and, in the course of his investigation, he had presumably met and attracted Ginnie – attracted her sufficiently to make her leave England and set up home with him in Agios Nikitas.

It made more sense that her employment as a tourist rep started while she was out on Corfu. Though just possible that she had taken the job in order to go and join Georgio, it was more likely that she had been recruited out there once she had mastered the language. There was little evidence that Georgio did much in the way of work, so no doubt whatever she earned was welcome.

Mrs Pargeter wished she knew more about Georgio. Though he seemed to spend much of his time drinking ouzo there, he was a rather shadowy figure round the taverna. She had not paid as much attention to him as to

Spiro, Sergeant Karaskakis and Yianni. But now he had definitely moved a few notches up her list of suspects.

And if Ginnie – whether willingly or unwillingly – was his accomplice, some other details fell into place. Mrs Pargeter recalled how the tour rep had insisted that first evening on taking them from Spiro's to the Villa Eleni by the curving route up the hillside, claiming it was less steep. And yet the next morning Mrs Pargeter had found the direct route no steeper than the other.

Wasn't it possible that Ginnie had taken them the long way to give someone time to set up the drugged drinks in the villa . . . ?

Theodosia. They had met Theodosia coming from the Villa Eleni. Was it she who had doctored the ouzo and the mineral water? If so, had she done it off her own bat or on someone else's orders?

Thinking of the mineral water raised another suspicion of Ginnie. Now Mrs Pargeter recalled the events of the evening, she remembered the English girl casting doubt on the purity of the villa's tap-water. And yet the *Berlitz Travel Guide* Mrs Pargeter had consulted before her holiday had, she now remembered, stated unequivocally that Corfu's tap-water was perfectly safe to drink. Wasn't it likely that Ginnie had only raised the anxiety to ensure that, if any water was drunk, it would be from the bottle she knew to be drugged?

Mrs Pargeter tried to envisage Ginnie in the rôle of murderer, but somehow the costume didn't fit. Maybe, given more information, it would.

And yet the girl was clearly involved. Through Georgio? That would make sense. If he dominated her to the extent that she allowed him to beat her up, she would presumably do whatever he told her. And if he told her to help him commit murder, presumably she'd go along with that too.

And yet what was Georgio's motive? What motive

could any of them have against Joyce Dover, widow of a Uruguayan former gun-runner?

Mrs Pargeter knew she had not yet got enough information to answer those questions. But at the same time she felt totally confident that she would get it. Self-doubt had never been one of her failings.

The one dominant impression that returned to her whenever she thought about the case was that she was up against a conspiracy. She had a sense that her quarry was not so much an individual as the entire community of Agios Nikitas. They were all related. They all, beneath their surface welcome and bonhomie towards the income-bearing tourists, retained a fierce, private individuality.

So if, say, Georgio was proved to be the murderer, there was no doubt that others had helped him set up his murder. Ginnie had delayed his victim's arrival at the Villa Eleni, Theodosia had planted the soporifics, and Sergeant Karaskakis had guaranteed the partiality of any investigation that might take place. There had probably been other accomplices too, like whoever had watered the villa's flowers and so efficiently swept away the murderer's traces.

Little bubbles of new thought kept rising in Mrs Pargeter's mind. Some of them interconnected to form bigger bubbles before bursting from insufficient information. But fresh thoughts rose to replace them.

Yes, thought Mrs Pargeter, I'm getting there.

31

Mrs Joan Frimley Wainwright, dressed in her beige dress, large cotton hat and sunglasses, had no trouble with Passport Control or Customs at Corfu Airport, and was met at the barrier by Larry Lambeth.

In spite of the darkness, the air was still fragrantly warm when they came out of the terminal. Because of the time difference, it was mid-evening in Corfu.

'Do you want to go straight back to Agios Nikitas?' asked Larry once they were safely in his car. 'Or stop over in Corfu Town like you said you would?'

Mrs Pargeter had forgotten that her London mission had been achieved in less time than had been allotted for the fictitious Paleokastritsa trip.

'I think I'd better go back there tonight. I want to try and get this thing sorted out before the suicide verdict's made official.'

'OK. What, straight to Agios Nikitas then – or have a bite to eat first? I know a great restaurant here in the town.'

'Well . . .' Mrs Pargeter replied cautiously. 'I did have a snack on the plane, but . . . Oh yes, let's go and eat. Then I can bring you up to date on what I found out in London.'

'And I can bring you up to date on what I've found out out here,' said Larry Lambeth.

The restaurant was not on the tourist beat, set unobtrusively in a backstreet of the Old Town, away from the waterfront and the Liston. The functional lighting, plain white tablecloths and lack of menus in any language but Greek bore witness to its gastronomic seriousness.

Mrs Pargeter and Larry had been to the kitchen and selected their main courses. Both were having *astakos*, the saltwater crayfish that is translated (incorrectly) on most menus as 'lobster'. Unflinching, they had witnessed the demise of their selections, plunged live into the boiling pot.

Now, as they nibbled on *dolmades* and olives, Mrs Pargeter filled Larry in on the results of Mrs Joan Frimley Wainwright's visit to London.

'Fact is,' he sighed when she'd finished, 'as one bit gets clearer, another bit gets muddier.'

'Yes. What do you know about Georgio, though?'

'Well – surprise, surprise – he's a cousin of Spiro, and of Stephano.'

'Who's Stephano? I haven't heard of him.'

'Oh, sorry. Stephano – Stephano Karaskakis. The Tourist Police Sergeant.'

'Right. I was never told his Christian name.'

'Anyway, Georgio is a bit of a no-hoper. Sits around drinking ouzo all day devising money-making schemes which either never get started or never make any money if they do get started. I think he's probably a bit jealous of Spiro having the taverna.'

'Spiro does well out of that?'

Larry Lambeth made a 'so-so' gesture. 'By Corfiot standards, anyway. Not that he makes any money out of Georgio. Or Stephano, come to that. They both eat and drink there all the time, but neither one has ever been seen to pay a single drachma for anything.'

'That's interesting. And Ginnie does live with Georgio, doesn't she?'

'Oh yes. Doesn't advertise the fact, mind you. Better the English punters think of her as single, unconnected with the locals.'

'They're not married?'

'No, no. Might be a bit of local opposition if he actually made it legal with a foreigner. No problems having one as a chattel, though.'

'And does he beat her up?'

'I'm sure he does. That type has to take his failure out on someone.'

'Hm. Did you know that Georgio had been to England?'

'Yes, I did, actually. Couple of years back. That was yet another of his money-making ideas.'

'Oh?'

'Fact is, Georgio was going to go over to England to buy one of those JCBs – you know, big earth-moving truck things. He was going to buy it, ship it back here and clean up by renting it out. Not such a daft idea, actually. There's always any amount of construction work going on, and lots of other stuff like shifting sand where they're making artificial beaches, clearing seaweed, all that.'

'But presumably that project didn't work out either?'

'No. Fact is, he never even bought it, did he? Probably hadn't got enough of the old mazooma, anyway – they're hellish expensive, those things. And no doubt when he got to London, he just drank his way through the money he had got.'

'Hm . . . And tried to investigate Chris Dover's business affairs . . . Now why on earth would he do that?'

'Well, knowing Georgio, he must have reckoned there was some profit in it for him.'

'But how could there be?'

'Search me, lady.'

32

Their main course arrived, garnished with a few boiled potatoes and a delectably pungent sauce. Larry Lambeth ordered more retsina and they devoted their full attention to the meal.

When her plate was just a pile of shell fragments, Mrs Pargeter dabbed at the corner of her mouth with a paper napkin and purred, 'That was delicious.'

'Told you this place was good.'

'Yes.' She took a long swallow of retsina. 'Larry, you said you'd found out some stuff too . . .'

'Right, Mrs Pargeter. Right, yes, I have. You know you asked me to get a bit of background on the whole Agios Nikitas set-up?'

'Yes.'

'Well, I done a bit of research, you know, asking around, and it seems like the tourist thing is comparatively new there.'

'How new?'

'Fact is, thirty years ago Agios Nikitas was just a little fishing village. The harbour obviously was there, otherwise just a few huts. Only people who lived there was the fishermen, and they went back to Agralias in the winters.'

'Was there a taverna?'

'Yes. Same building as there is now, but very primitive. Run by Spiro's old man.'

'Also called Spiro.'

'Right. Pretty safe guess most of the time out here. Anyway, reason I'm concentrating on that time is there was something odd happened then.'

'Odd?'

'An unexplained death. Body never found.'

'Oh? Who died?'

'Well . . . Look, I better give you a bit more background on the whole Karaskakis family bit.'

'Stephano, you mean?'

'He comes into it, but not just Stephano. They're all called Karaskakis round here, you see . . . Spiro, Georgio,Theodosia, Yianni – they're all Karaskakises.'

'Oh.' Mrs Pargeter looked thoughtful.

'Anyway, old Spiro's wife had died young . . . Complications on the birth when she had Theodosia, I think. Fairly primitive medical facilities back in those days. And, time I'm talking about – 1959, round then – old Spiro's sick, too . . . dying of cancer, as it turned out, though it wasn't diagnosed at the time. Anyway, he's worried about what's going to happen to the taverna. Tourist business just starting to build up on the island, you see, and, though it hasn't hit Agios Nikitas in a big way yet, the old man can see that his little taverna's a potential gold-mine. Trouble is, though, Spiro – young Spiro, you know, the one who owns it now – he's not that interested. He's round fifteen and really likes school, touch of the old academic, wants to go to university, that kind of number. Well, old Spiro won't hear of this, wants the taverna to stay in the family and he doesn't trust his other son to run it.'

'Other son?' Mrs Pargeter echoed.

'Right. They're twins, you see. Spiro's the good one, but Christo is a bit of a tearaway.'

'Christo? Did you say Christo?'

'Yes. That's the other son's name. Identical twins they was.'

'Of course,' Mrs Pargeter murmured.

'Anyway, this Christo hangs around with a bad crowd – including, incidentally, his cousins Georgio and Stephano – and, though he's very interested in getting the taverna 'cause he reckons there's money in it, old Spiro doesn't trust him. He's determined that, whether the boy wants to or not, the older twin Spiro's going to take over the family business.'

'So who died?' Mrs Pargeter asked softly.

Larry Lambeth rubbed his chin reflectively. 'There's a lot of different versions of exactly what happened, but it was Christo. Killed in an accident on a boat.'

'How?'

'Story goes, Christo and his cousins—'

'Georgio and Stephano?'

'That's right. Anyway, they stole a boat. Dinghy with an outboard – someone along the coast had bought a few of them to rent out to the tourists. So they nick this thing, but apparently the outboard's dodgy – it blows up, the boat catches fire, sinks – and Christo is never seen again.'

'Missing, presumed drowned?'

'That's it.'

'But what about Georgio and Stephano? Why weren't they hurt? How did they escape?'

'Well, by coincidence, they aren't on the boat when the outboard blows. Christo has just dropped them off at the harbour, he goes out for a little joyride on his own and – boof!' Larry's hands opened out, miming the explosion.

'Was there any suggestion at the time that the boat might have been sabotaged?'

'Certainly was. More than that, there was the suggestion that Christo was sabotaging it himself when it blew up.'

'An own goal? You mean he was making a booby-trap for someone else?'

'You got it, Mrs P. Care to make any guesses who he was planning to bump off?'

'Spiro,' Mrs Pargeter murmured.

'That was the rumour that went around at the time, yes.'

'But it went wrong . . .'

'Right, Christo hoist with his own whatsit.'

'So, with his brother dead and his father dying, Spiro had no choice but to take over the taverna?'

'Yes. Old man dies soon after, Spiro has to put aside his intellectual aspirations, like, and buckle down to running the family business. Does all right out of it, and all.'

Mrs Pargeter was silent as the avalanche of her thoughts gathered momentum.

'So, anyway,' Larry concluded, 'got *two* unexplained deaths to think about now, haven't we, Mrs P.? I always remember something that your old man once said. "The explanation for a murder often lies in a previous murder." You ever heard him say that?'

'No,' she replied rather primly. Murder was not a subject that had ever come up in her conversations with the late Mr Pargeter.

'Well, I reckon odds are,' said Larry, 'that there's got to be some connection between Joyce Dover's death and Christo Karaskakis' death back in 1959.'

'Assuming, of course,' said Mrs Pargeter quietly, 'that that was when he died.'

33

It was Greek party night at Spiro's when they got back to Agios Nikitas. The tourists who had paid for the evening's entertainment had eaten up their cheese pies and barbecued lamb and were now vigorously applauding the dancing.

As Mrs Pargeter and Larry Lambeth arrived, Spiro

and Yianni, side by side, arms locked on each other's shoulders, were solemnly following the ritual of long-remembered steps, while the live group of bouzouki, guitar and drums built up the pace of their music. There was a pagan magnificence about the two men, Yianni justifying the cliché description of a young Greek god, and Spiro more solid but still impressive and surprisingly light-footed for his bulk. Both their faces were rigid with the concentration of the dance.

Their audience clapped along with the pounding beat. Mr Safari Suit was arranging Mrs Safari Suit in a suitable foreground pose for his next snap. Linda from South Woodham Ferrers was arguing with Keith from South Woodham Ferrers over whether it had been a good idea to bring Craig with them. The little boy evidently didn't think a lot of Greek dancing and was bawling his head off. Linda wanted to take him back to the villa, but Keith insisted that they'd paid for the evening and they were jolly well going to get their money's worth. An atmosphere had developed between the couple. Keith said in some ways it'd be quite a relief to get back to the office.

The Secretary with Short Bleached Hair and the Secretary with Long Bleached Hair lingered on the edge of the dancing area, eager for all this male display dancing to end and for the disco music to start. Their suntans had settled down a little; five days into their package, they looked proudly browner than that day's air freight delivery of white-skinned English.

Mrs Pargeter and Larry found a vacant table, but it was some time before they could order a drink, as the masculine *pas de deux* gave way to a dance with brightly-coloured scarves which involved all of the taverna's waiters.

Mrs Pargeter watched Spiro leading the dance with a preoccupied, automatic jollity, and thought perhaps now she knew some of the reasons for the underlying melancholy of his dark face.

The scarf dance ended. The audience, convinced they were getting an exclusive taste of the authentic Greece (just as the party night audience at the taverna did every Monday), clapped enthusiastically. After perfunctory bows, the dancers moved back into waiter mode and hurried towards the many hands that waved for drinks.

Yianni appeared at their table. 'Please, I get you drinks, yes, please?'

Larry ordered retsina and brandy, but, rather than rushing off to get them, the waiter lingered. 'Please, you see Conchita, please?'

'Sorry, I've only just come back here. Been away for a couple of days.'

'She say she come to party night. I not see her, please.'

His black eyes looked so moist and desolate that Mrs Pargeter had to say something to reassure him. 'She'll turn up. Don't worry, it's early yet.'

As the waiter slouched disconsolately back into the taverna, she felt very sorry for him. Dear, oh dear, had Conchita fulfilled her ambitions for a purely physical relationship, and had Yianni now served his purpose and been cast aside? Conchita gave the impression of being a tough, modern cookie. Nothing in Yianni's culture or background could have prepared him – or any Greek man – for the novel experience of being used as a sex-object.

Recorded disco music started up, current British chart successes alternating with banal Euro-hits. The Secretary with Short Bleached Hair and the Secretary with Long Bleached Hair moved keenly into the dancing area where, to their great delight, they were quickly joined by two young men in fluorescent T-shirts and cycling shorts.

Mrs Pargeter sipped her retsina and took in the scene. Larry Lambeth, seeing that she was deep in thought, respected her silence.

She was convinced now that Christo Karaskakis had escaped from the burning boat which was believed to have killed him, and that its flames almost definitely explained the scarring on his face . . .

Yes! Another detail slotted into place. She remembered how Mr Fisher-Metcalf had started to respond to the overexposed photograph of Spiro. That must have been because Spiro's face, with the distinctive features smoothed out, looked very much like the scarred face of his identical twin, the solicitor's client.

She was now in no doubt that Chris Dover and Christo Karaskakis had been one and the same person.

34

She forced her mind back to Christo's escape from the boat. Somehow he must have found his way to England, probably arriving at Dover, then changed his name and set out to make a career in his new country.

He had taken the decision to obscure his real origins and make himself as British as he could be. But, until he perfected the language, he needed some explanation of his accent. How he had come to select Uruguay as a fictitious background there was no way of knowing, but it had been an inspired choice. The British as a nation tend to lump all foreigners together, anyway, but the number who could conduct an intelligent conversation about any aspect of Uruguay is so tiny as to be unworthy of consideration. The number who know anything about the country's politics is even tinier, and so Chris Dover's references to political disagreements and even implications of torture would never have been questioned.

Now this major breach had been made in the wall of logic, other details came tumbling through at a rush. Mrs Pargeter knew why she hadn't at first recognised Conchita sitting at Spiro's. The girl looked so natural there because it was the natural place for her to be. Though neither side knew it, she had been sitting amongst her family.

Another realisation came through. The reason why Chris Dover had deliberately avoided meeting Hamish Ramon Henriques was simply because he didn't dare come face to face with a native Spanish-speaker. Such an encounter would almost inevitably lead to exposure of the lies he had invented about his Uruguayan upbringing.

But the question Mrs Pargeter could not yet answer was why Christo Karaskakis had created this huge subterfuge, what had driven him so thoroughly to disguise the truth about himself – even to the extent of landing his daughter with the unlikely name of Conchita, for God's sake!

There were two possible explanations for such extreme behaviour – it could be a reaction either of guilt or of fear.

If Christo Karaskakis had committed some dreadful crime in Agios Nikitas, then guilt might have forced him to flee from the dangers of discovery and retribution. Sabotaging the outboard motor – if it were definitely known that that was what he was doing when it blew up in his face – might well qualify as such a crime.

Alternatively, though, perhaps he was the intended victim of the sabotage.

This theory appealed to Mrs Pargeter a lot more than the other one.

Under those circumstances, Christo Karaskakis might have been so frightened by the incident in the burning boat that he fled from Corfu and made himself unrecognisable to escape further attempts on his life. Perhaps he had spent his whole life in fear that the person who had so nearly killed him in 1959 would not rest until the job had been completed.

So who could have sabotaged the boat nearly thirty years before?

The people known to be involved were Georgio and Stephano.

Presumably Spiro had been around at the time, too.

But Spiro did seem a pretty unlikely suspect, because he had nothing to gain from his brother's death. Indeed, he had quite a lot to lose. His dreams of the academic life were still just about alive while there was a chance of Christo reforming to such a point that old Spiro thought him worthy of taking on the family business. But, with his brother dead, young Spiro was condemned to burying his hopes for ever.

The other two made much more appealing suspects. Georgio had actually gone to London looking for Chris Dover, and Stephano – Sergeant Karaskakis – had been shameless in diverting suspicion about Joyce's death. Because, following her new logic, Mrs Pargeter now felt certain that the same person who had attempted to murder Christo had succeeded in murdering Joyce, presumably to stop her from exposing the first crime.

But which of her two suspects was the murderer?

Mrs Pargeter looked across the taverna's dancing area to the little table under the window where Georgio sat drinking ouzo with some cronies. The man seemed such an incompetent that it was hard to visualise him planning murder. But when it came to crime, as the late Mr Pargeter had frequently remarked, appearances can be terribly deceptive.

Sergeant Karaskakis certainly made a more obvious suspect. He was confident, calculating and in his eye at times there burned a light of pure evil.

Mrs Pargeter looked over towards the taverna doorway and saw the object of her speculation talking to Spiro.

They were in exactly the same positions that they had been in when Joyce saw them the evening she died, Spiro with his back to her and the Sergeant visible over his shoulder.

Another possibility slotted into place. Maybe it hadn't been the Sergeant who had prompted Joyce's panic. Perhaps it had been the sight of Spiro's backview, identical to that of her late husband. If that had been the case, Joyce's looking as if she had seen a ghost had been almost literally appropriate.

Immediately Mrs Pargeter recalled the second time her friend had panicked. Inside the taverna. When she saw Theodosia over the bar counter.

Fiercely excited, Mrs Pargeter rose to her feet and, unaware of Larry Lambeth's curious look, rushed towards the taverna entrance.

Sergeant Karaskakis saw her approach and deliberately stood in her way. 'Mrs Pargeter,' he said.

'Yes'

'The Tourist Police keep records of where all visitors to our island are staying.'

'Oh?' She looked up at him, all innocence.

'There is no record of your having stayed in a hotel in Corfu Town or in Paleokastritsa last night.'

Mrs Pargeter smiled. 'Isn't that dreadful? People are so inefficient these days, aren't they? You'd think it was a simple enough thing to keep proper records, but for some people even that's too much trouble.'

Sergeant Karaskakis wasn't fooled by her bluff and she knew it. He held her in a long stare, which was undisguisedly threatening. Mrs Pargeter continued to smile her defiance up at him, but she felt a little trickle of fear in the small of her back.

After a moment, he drew curtly to one side, and let her pass through into the building.

She stood exactly where Joyce had stood, and looked exactly where Joyce had looked.

Theodosia was not behind the bar this time.

There was nobody behind the bar.

But directly in Mrs Pargeter's eyeline was the enshrined photograph.

The photograph of old Spiro. Of the person Larry Lambeth would have described as Christo Karaskakis' 'old man'.

'If you want to find out, the explanation for everything will be found behind the old man's p—'

'Photograph'?

35

'Ah, it's locked. That's good.' Larry Lambeth's whisper was gentle on the night air.

'Good?' Mrs Pargeter echoed. 'Why good?'

'Because it means no one's here. Often during the season Spiro sleeps in the taverna rather than going back to Agralias – particularly if he's been late after a party night. But the fact that it's locked means he's gone home.'

'Will you be able to get in all right?'

He laughed at the idea that she had even asked the question. 'No problem. Not that much choice of padlocks available here on the island.'

He fished a bunch of keys out of the pocket of his shorts and started testing them. Mrs Pargeter, hunched in the shadow under the taverna awning, looked nervously about her. The darkness was total, but in Agios Nikitas she could never fully relax into a feeling of being unobserved.

What they were doing, she knew, was risky, but she was determined to follow through her latest theory. And Larry Lambeth, of course, gave her unquestioning cooperation. He would have done anything – laid down his life without a murmur, if required – for the widow of the late Mr Pargeter.

She hugged the brown-paper-wrapped package that – in what seemed like another life – Joyce Dover had given her at Gatwick Airport. At least now she knew what it contained. And what the contents were for.

There was a click as the padlock's tumblers turned. Larry Lambeth pushed the glass doors open and gestured Mrs Pargeter to follow him in. Safely inside, he clicked on the thin beam of a pencil torch.

There was no prevarication. Both knew exactly what they were looking for and crossed to behind the bar. Larry climbed adroitly on to the counter, reached up and unhooked the enshrined photograph from its niche.

Mrs Pargeter remembered Spiro's proud words. 'My father. It was taken just before he died – thirty years ago – but still he keeps an eye on his taverna. Spiro brings good luck to Spiro. The photograph keeps away the Evil Eye.'

Larry Lambeth put the picture face down on the counter and handed Mrs Pargeter the torch. She trained it on the back of the frame as he brushed off dust and cobwebs. Deftly he slid a knifeblade through the brown paper tape that held the mount in place, then lifted out the rectangular cardboard backing.

'On this or the photograph itself, do you reckon?'

'The photograph,' she breathed.

He eased out the thick sheet and placed it, blank side upward, on the counter. Mrs Pargeter was ready, the ouzo bottle opened and a paper duster bunched over its top.

Their breathing was fast and shallow. Larry Lambeth

nodded. She upended the bottle, felt the duster fill and moisten, then squeezed out the excess fluid.

Her eyes met Larry's for a second before she made the first firm wipe across the back of the photograph.

For a moment, nothing seemed to happen. Maybe there was nothing there . . . Or maybe the effect of the chemical had simply worn off over the years . . . The whole edifice of conjecture and connection she had built up swayed and threatened to topple.

Then, mercifully, the first purplish streaks showed and quickly the swathe of card she had wiped was marked with spidery Greek lettering.

Involuntary sighs of relief burst from both of them.

Confident now, Mrs Pargeter wiped another stripe across. And another and another, until the entire rectangle had been covered.

Her efforts were rewarded by more lettering. 'What does it say, Larry? What does it say?'

He translated what he read fluently but slowly, draining all emotion from his voice.

' "I write this, knowing that I will soon be dead, but I do not wish to die without recording the act of evil that I have witnessed. I write this in sadness and in hatred, and that hatred is for my own flesh and blood.

' "Christo, you have committed an offence that can never be forgiven. You have tried to kill your own brother by sabotaging the outboard motor on the boat you stole. I know that you had help from Stephano in your evil plan, but he is weak and does whatever you tell him. The outrage was your idea and you must bear the full responsibility of it.

'"Spiro told me what happened. He is here with me now. Spiro, who is so clever at his studies, has shown me how to write this so that you will never find it.

'"When I die, which as I said will not be long away, I will die hating you, Christo, more than ever father hated son. You have brought shame on our family and you will carry my curse upon you till the end of your life. Your death will be violent and terrifying – you will feel the fear you tried to inflict on your brother. You tried to kill by fire one whom you should have respected above all others, and so by fire you will yourself die. The day may come soon, or it may be many years away, but the fire will catch you eventually. That is a father's curse, a curse spoken in the name of St Spiridon. And though you try to hide behind a new name, my dying curse will still find you out to destroy you, Christo." And it's signed "Spiro Karaskakis".'

Mrs Pargeter was about to speak, but a terrible sound froze the words on her lips.

It was just recognisably human, a voice that screamed in pain like a trapped animal.

36

Larry Lambeth shot across the room towards the source of the sound. Mrs Pargeter was a little behind him and stood in the doorway to the kitchen, looking at the sight illuminated by his narrow torch-beam.

Theodosia was crouched like a cornered animal on the rough pallet which served her as a bed. Her scream had subsided to a feral whimpering, and her usually impassive face was ravaged by tears.

Larry Lambeth snapped some questions at her in Greek, which reinforced the strength of her sobbing.

'Be gentle with her,' murmured Mrs Pargeter, as she moved across the room towards the terrified woman. She sat on the pallet and put a plump arm round the quivering shoulders.

Theodosia's first instinct was to flinch as if to break away, but Mrs Pargeter's stroking hands and soothing but uncomprehended words gradually brought calm. The pace of the sobbing slowed, and the woman's head sank down on to her comforter's shoulder. Mrs Pargeter could feel the warm dampness of tears through the thin cotton of her dress.

'She's a witness of what we done,' said Larry Lambeth twitchily. 'She'll tell Stephano and Georgio and that lot.'

'She can't tell them. She can't speak.'

'She has ways of communication.'

As if taking his words as a cue, Theodosia suddenly let out a different sound. A strange, unearthly sound, that seemed to come from deep within her, torn painfully from her frame.

It took a moment before Mrs Pargeter realised that the woman was speaking.

The voice was rasping and rusty, but with an incongruously innocent lightness. Through its strangeness, it was the voice of a child, the child Theodosia had been the last time she had spoken, before experiencing the shock which had struck her dumb for thirty years.

'What is she saying?' whispered Mrs Pargeter urgently.

'She says that she heard me read her father's curse. It frightens her very much.'

More strange sounds were dragged from Theodosia's body.

Larry Lambeth interpreted. 'She did not know that Christo had deliberately sabotaged the boat. She saw the fire. It was terrible.'

Theodosia mouthed hopelessly, once again robbed of speech by this recollection. Mrs Pargeter felt sure it must have been the sight of her brother apparently going up in flames that had traumatised her all those years before.

But the woman regained control and once again the uneven, unaccustomed speech began.

'She hates her brother now she knows the truth. She adds her curse to her father's curse. She hopes he will die.'

Too late, thought Mrs Pargeter. That merciful tumour on the brain of Christo Karaskakis – or Chris Dover – had saved him from the literal fulfilment of old Spiro's curse. But who knew what flames of conscience had scorched him at the moment of his death?

Or, though she didn't really believe in hell, she could recognise that the idea of Chris Dover roasting there for all eternity would neatly tie up all the ends of his story.

A new urgency came into Theodosia's voice.

'She says they've got the girl.'

'Girl?' Mrs Pargeter echoed. 'Conchita?'

Yes, of course. At the time she had seen nothing odd in Conchita's non-appearance at Spiro's Greek party, putting it down to some tiff between the girl and Yianni. But now the absence took on more sinister colouring. And that had been late evening. Conchita could have been missing for up to seven hours.

Larry Lambeth's translation confirmed her worst fears. 'The dark-haired English girl, she says.'

'Who's got her?'

He urgently relayed the question to Theodosia.

'The tourist woman – that must be Ginnie – the tourist woman arranged to meet her on the headland, but Stephano and Georgio were waiting there, and they took the girl.'

'Oh no!' Mrs Pargeter could not forget the reference to Stephano in old Spiro's deposition. Stephano had aided and abetted Christo in the earlier crime. Christo was dead, but Sergeant Karaskakis was still very much alive and very dangerous. 'Where have they taken her?'

The translation came back quickly. 'There's an old

fisherman's hut on the headland. They've got her in there.'

Mrs Pargeter grabbed Larry Lambeth's hand. 'Come on! We must get there – quickly! There have already been too many deaths in Agios Nikitas!'

37

The headland referred to was one of the scrub-covered arms that encircled the bay of Agios Nikitas. It was a steep-sided spine of rock, the end of which thousands of years before had dropped away into the sea to form cliffs. There were a couple of paths across the ridge which led to tiny bays otherwise accessible only by boat, but they were little used. The thorny undergrowth was inimical to travellers in the tourist uniform of shorts and T-shirts, and the gradient unappealing in the daytime sun.

Heat raised no problems for Mrs Pargeter and Larry Lambeth, but the steep climb and the sharp thorns did. They were both scratched and breathless by the time they approached the dilapidated hut. The darkness was diluted by a thin sliver of moon and their eyes had quickly accommodated to the conditions.

'I'll go first,' Larry murmured.

There had been a path to the door in the days when fishermen used the building regularly, but this now showed only as an indentation in the surrounding scrub, which muscled up close, threatening to engulf the hut. No light showed through the broken glass of the windows, and the only sound was the incessant restlessness of the sea.

Larry moved cautiously forward to the door, found the

handle and pushed it inward with a sudden movement. He paused, but, the silence remaining unbroken, moved forward and was lost in the darkness of the interior.

There were two sounds. A soft thud. A harder thud.

Then silence reasserted itself.

Whatever dangers lay inside the hut, Mrs Pargeter had come too far to shirk them. It was no time for pussyfooting. Her dead friend's daughter was in danger.

Coolly, Mrs Pargeter pushed through the encroaching brushwood and in through the open door. As she did so, she announced in a clear voice, 'Good morning. I am Mrs Pargeter and I am coming in to see what's happening.'

The darkness she entered was total. Her feet stepped firmly across the floor of dusty rock.

There was a loud clatter behind her as the door was slammed shut. She turned, to be met by the dazzling beam of a flashlight.

'You are a very nosey woman, Mrs Pargeter,' said a voice she recognised.

'With some justification, I think . . .' she said, 'Sergeant Karaskakis.'

38

Now she could see the rectangular outline of his uniform against the wall of the hut. His face was in shadow, but she could supply for herself the evil leer beneath that triangular moustache.

She turned to look round the hut. Conchita was tied to an old wooden chair, which had in turn been tied to one of the hut's upright supports. Though the girl strained to communicate, only a liquid gurgle could penetrate the gag made by her own scarf, whose overpaid designer had never envisaged this usage for his creation.

Larry Lambeth lay face downward, unmoving, on the floor. Mrs Pargeter rushed to his side.

'It's all right. He's only unconscious,' said Sergeant Karaskakis languidly, as he hooked the flashlight to an overhead beam.

Mrs Pargeter turned Larry over. His eyes did not react, but his breathing was regular. She looked up to the Sergeant, who loomed above her, gently tapping against his palm the nightstick which had presumably knocked Larry out.

'As I say, you are very nosey. Foolishly nosey. Too nosey for your own good, Mrs Pargeter.'

She stood up and faced him, remembering more of the late Mr Pargeter's words of wisdom. 'The only situation which might justify panic is one in which panic is likely to help. Such a situation never arises. Though pretended panic may sometimes cause a useful diversion, real panic can never be anything other than a waste of energy.'

'I do know, Sergeant,' she said, 'why all this is happening. It is the crime of Christo Karaskakis that is behind it all.'

He stiffened at the mention of the name.

'And Joyce Dover was killed because it was feared that she might reveal the secrets of that crime. Which was nonsense. She had no desire to expose anyone. All she wanted to do was to find out about her husband's past. All his life Chris had managed to keep the truth about his background secret, but his conscience would not allow him to let that secret die with him. In what was perhaps a final gesture of honesty, he offered his wife the chance of knowing the truth. He saw to it that she received a letter after his death. And that letter led her here to Agios Nikitas.'

Sergeant Karaskakis casually pulled a sheet of paper out of his pocket. 'Might this be what you are speaking of?'

Even in that inadequate lighting, Mrs Pargeter could see the distinctively purple writing on one side of the paper.

'Yes. You found that in Joyce's luggage at the Villa Eleni.'

'So?' he asked insolently, shoving the letter back into his pocket.

So . . . that means you were definitely there the night she was murdered. But Mrs Pargeter didn't bother to say it out loud.

'Everything you say,' the Sergeant continued, 'may be very interesting . . . but I don't know what relevance it has to me.'

'It is relevant to you because you were involved in Christo's original crime. You and Georgio helped him steal the boat, you helped him sabotage the outboard motor. You were an accessory to the attempted murder that went so horribly wrong.'

'You've done a lot of research, Mrs Pargeter,' he said, without intonation of either praise or blame.

'Yes. Where's Georgio?' she asked suddenly.

The Sergeant smiled. 'He has gone home. Gone home with his English whore to get drunk. Georgio was always feeble. He can't stand it when things get too hot. Thirty years ago, he was with us when we stole the boat, but when we start to fix the outboard, he gets afraid and goes away. He is not a man, Georgio.'

Mrs Pargeter was pleased that Sergeant Karaskakis made no attempt to deny his crime. But her pleasure was not unmingled with other emotions. His ready admission of guilt suggested that he was not too worried by the possibility of her surviving to bear witness against him. She knew she must try and keep him talking as long as possible, while her mind desperately raced to see a way out of her predicament.

'Sergeant, there was no need to kill Joyce Dover. She represented no threat to you. And there is certainly no need to harm Conchita. You should release her.'

'No.'

'Then at least take the gag off. No one can hear her shouting out here.'

'No. She talks too much,' he said, affronted. 'She talks rudely. She does not behave as a woman should behave.'

It was not the moment to enter into a feminist debate, so Mrs Pargeter asked coolly, 'What are you planning to do with her then? With all of us, come to that?'

'What happened with the boat,' he began slowly, 'has been a secret for thirty years. We want it to remain a secret for ever.'

'Fine,' said Mrs Pargeter. 'That suits us fine. We don't want to dig up the past. When we get back to England, we'll never think about it again, promise. I can assure you, your little crime may seem pretty important out here in Agios Nikitas, but the rest of the world has no interest in it at all.'

'We cannot take risks, I'm afraid. Christo would not wish such risks to be taken.'

'You shouldn't still care what Christo thinks. Show a bit of independence. Make a decision of your own for once in your life.'

This approach did not unfortunately have the desired effect; Sergeant Karaskakis seemed instead to read it as a challenge to his masculinity. 'Don't you dare speak to me like that! Or I will gag you like the other one!'

'Gagging me won't help you at all.'

'It will, Mrs Pargeter. So will tying you up.'

As he spoke, he reached behind him for a hank of rope. She struggled, but a woman in her late sixties was no match for a man more than ten years younger. Her arms were quickly trussed behind her and she was strapped against another upright beam beside Conchita.

'All right, well done,' she taunted him. 'So you've managed to knock out one man from behind and tie up two women. What do you want – a medal for bravery?'

'Mrs Pargeter,' he sneered, 'your death is one that I will not regret at all.'

'Oh, I see.' She was still managing – with some difficulty – to keep the insolence in her voice. 'And how are you proposing that I should be killed?'

He gave her a smile, though there was no vestige of humour in it. 'This is a very dry island in the summer. There are many fires. A wooden building like this would not survive long in a fire.'

Conchita gurgled and struggled as she heard this spelling out of their fate, but Mrs Pargeter still contrived to appear unruffled, even though she had just noticed two petrol cans against the wall behind the Sergeant. 'Fires do get investigated, you know. If you're proposing to use that petrol, traces would be left. Arson is a fairly simple crime to recognise.'

'So? There is a lot of arson on the island already. Men from other villages may be jealous of Agios Nikitas' success with the tourist trade. They will be blamed. As I say, there are many such crimes. It would not be thought strange.'

'But some of the details might be thought strange. The fact that two of the charred bodies had been tied up is the kind of thing that might be noticed.'

His mirthless smile grew broader. 'That would depend, of course, on who was conducting the investigation. I represent the authorities here in Agios Nikitas. I would be the first person on the scene of the tragedy.'

'So you reckon you could tamper with the evidence again – just as you did after Joyce's death?'

He shrugged.

His next words were more chilling than anything he had said up until that point. 'Mind you, it would probably be simpler if the bodies were found *not* tied up . . .'

'You mean dead before the fire got to them?'

'Why not?' Once again he tapped his nightstick against his palm. He looked across at the two women, assessing his next move.

Mrs Pargeter was not a religious woman. She was not convinced that God existed, and so her philosophy had always been to enjoy this life to the full, in case the concept of a future life was merely misleading propaganda circulated to control the worst excesses of public behaviour. But she prayed at that moment.

And, as Sergeant Karaskakis advanced towards her with his nightstick upraised, her prayer was answered.

The door burst open.

'No, Stephano! Don't do it!'

Framed in the doorway against the first paleness of dawn stood Spiro.

39

Sergeant Karaskakis lowered his weapon, subdued by the presence of a personality stronger than his own. He was silent, awaiting orders.

Mrs Pargeter couldn't understand in detail what orders Spiro gave him, but they seemed to be of the 'Go outside, I'll deal with you later' variety. The Sergeant, with the bad grace of a cat who's just had its mouse emancipated, slunk out of the hut into the grey dawn.

'Goodness,' said Mrs Pargeter, 'am I glad to see you, Spiro! That was quite a close shave. Do you know, he was proposing to set fire to the headland around us?'

Spiro shook his head, his dark eyes more melancholy than ever. 'Stephano is a dangerous and careless fool.'

'Yes.' Mrs Pargeter was suddenly garrulous with relief. 'I do know all about what happened,' she said.

Spiro looked puzzled.

'In 1959,' she explained. 'I know about the attempt to kill you, the way the outboard motor was sabotaged. And I know how it went wrong, and how Christo got hoist with his own petard, and how he got burnt and escaped to England and pretended to have come from Uruguay . . .'

Spiro still looked uncomprehending.

'Of course, you wouldn't have heard about any of that. Don't worry about it. The main thing is that I know why Joyce was killed and I know who killed her. And I've found out all about the curse your father put on Christo.'

'Curse?'

'Yes. I found it written on the back of the photograph – you know, in phenolphthalein.' The look of incomprehension in his face was now such that she explained, 'Maybe it's got a different name in Greek, but it's that stuff that's used as an indicator in chemistry, you know, to show the degree of alkaline or acidic content of . . .'

Her words drained away as she realised how little they meant to him. He did not understand even the most rudimentary details about chemistry.

And with that knowledge, she felt a whole sequence of other facts slot into place. Spiro had been the studious one who enjoyed chemistry, Christo the tearaway who wanted to own the taverna. But Chris Dover, presumed to be Christo, was the one who always wrote his secret correspondence in phenolphthalein.

Suddenly she saw a different perspective on the thirty-year-old 'accident' with the outboard motor. It was not an 'own goal' which had blown up in the perpetrator's face. It had injured – though not killed – the person for whom it had been intended.

And old Spiro's words, 'though you try to hide behind a new name', did not, as she had assumed, refer to Christo Karaskakis' adoption of the pseudonym 'Chris Dover'. They referred to Christo Karaskakis' usurpation of the name of his older brother, Spiro.

Chris Dover had not run away and changed his identity to escape the consequences of any crime he had committed. It had been to escape another attack from his homicidal brother, Christo.

And, once Spiro had fled to England, Christo had calmly taken over the identity of his identical twin, together with the taverna that he had always set his heart on owning.

The new Spiro had been confident that no one would reveal his secret. The real Spiro was too frightened of him to risk his anger again. Their father had died almost immediately after the incident, his death no doubt hastened by the knowledge of his young son's true nature. Their nine-year-old sister, Theodosia, had been traumatised into silence by witnessing the crime.

And, as for Stephano and Georgio, they were so totally the new Spiro's creatures that they represented no threat. So long as he gave them both unlimited and never to be recovered credit at the taverna, they'd keep their mouths shut.

Christo, now called Spiro, had achieved his ambition and was free to concentrate on making money out of his ill-gotten inheritance.

The facts were undeniable, but Mrs Pargeter tried to pretend they weren't. 'Well, I think you can untie us now, can't you, Spiro?' she said easily.

The implacable darkness of his eyes confirmed how forlorn her hope had been. For the first time since she had arrived on Corfu, Mrs Pargeter thought perhaps she understood the meaning of the expression 'the Evil Eye'.

'Why did you kill Joyce?' she asked.

'She was in my way,' he replied shortly.

'But how?'

'My brother was a rich man.'

'You mean you hope to inherit his money . . . ?'

Spiro did not reply, but Mrs Pargeter knew she had stumbled on the truth. All Spiro's crimes had the same motivation. His first attempt to kill his brother had been to inherit the taverna. Now he was trying once again to take what was not his.

'Was it Georgio who told you he was still alive?'

Spiro nodded. 'He was in London. He saw this man Chris Dover by chance in the street, he saw the likeness. He phoned me up to tell me.'

'And you told him to find out how much Chris Dover was worth?'

This earned another nod.

'But, if you were after his money, why didn't you make another attempt to kill your brother?'

'I think about it, but it is difficult from here. Then I hear he has died, anyway. Even better, next I hear his wife is coming out here. And then his daughter follows.'

Conchita whimpered as she took in the implication of what he was saying.

Spiro let out an unpleasant laugh and opened his hands in a gesture of satisfaction. 'St Spiridon helps all Spiros.'

'But you're not a real Spiro.'

'I am now. I might as well be.'

'Listen,' said Mrs Pargeter firmly. 'You've got something horribly wrong in all this, and that is the idea that you'll ever be able to prove you're related to your brother. Chris Dover covered his tracks so thoroughly that you don't stand a chance.'

'I'll do it,' Spiro insisted doggedly.

'You won't. So, for heaven's sake, stop this ridiculous business now. Joyce has already been killed for money that you're never going to see – and nothing can be done about that – but stop now before you harm Conchita.'

'I am going to inherit my brother's money.'

Mrs Pargeter looked into those dark eyes and saw no glimmer of hope at all. All that glowed in them was greed, an all-consuming peasant greed which was not susceptible to logic or argument. It was an obsession, a kind of madness, and a madness that could kill.

'Don't do it,' she appealed. 'Remember we are human beings. Just for a moment, think of Conchita and me as human beings.'

Spiro said nothing, but, pausing only to pick up the two petrol cans, walked out of the hut.

40

Mrs Pargeter had contemplated the possibility of death many times. It was a prospect which caused her anger rather than anguish. She had a great taste for life and wanted as large a helping of it as could be cajoled out of the Great Dinnerlady in the Sky.

The idea that her life was about to end was deeply unappealing. Though aware that her happiest days – those spent in the company of the late Mr Pargeter – were probably past, there were still a great many things she wanted to do, a great many experiences she wanted to cram in before that final shutter fell.

Though she had survived close calls in the past, this time there really did seem little she could do to ameliorate her situation. Larry Lambeth still showed no signs of movement and he was not near enough for her to test whether a jogging toe might rouse him.

She was also now disconcertingly aware of the stiff breeze that came directly off the sea and found a route through the broken windows of the hut. Nor was she reassured by the glimpsed sight, through the thin light of morning, of Spiro and Sergeant Karaskakis up-ending petrol cans over the scrub some hundred yards away on the seaward side. Once the match was dropped, it would be a matter of seconds before the flames reached the tinder-dry hut.

Annoyance still remained her dominant emotion. Death by fire was not her preferred mode of exit from the life she so fervently embraced. Joan of Arc had never figured as one of her heroines. Self-centred, silly adolescent girl, in Mrs Pargeter's view. Nowadays it wouldn't have been hearing voices; she'd have drawn attention to herself by anorexia nervosa.

These angry musings were interrupted by a sound from Conchita, and Mrs Pargeter realised that, through the restrictions of her gag, the poor girl was trying to scream. Dear oh dear, thought Mrs Pargeter, I'm being very selfish here. I have at least worked out a philosophy about death. I've thought it through, while this poor kid's only in her twenties, she can't feel there's been enough in her life yet to justify a premature departure from it. I must reassure her.

'Don't worry, Conchita, it'll be all right,' she said meaninglessly.

Suddenly there was a low line of flame in front of the outlines of Spiro and Stephano, and within seconds all the view from the windows had turned angry orange. The match had been dropped.

The terrified sounds from behind Conchita's gag redoubled in intensity. Time perhaps, Mrs Pargeter thought, for a tactical lie. If she could only calm the girl and keep her cheerful for a couple of minutes, it would all be over. The smoke in that enclosed place would probably asphyxiate them before they felt the real force of the flames.

'It's all right, love,' she reassured, with no basis of truth whatsoever. 'Larry had warned Yianni we were coming up here. He's waiting nearby. He'll save us.'

This did something to steady Conchita, though of course it didn't comfort Mrs Pargeter much. Nor did the flames racing towards the hut, grotesquely parodying the warmth and brightness by which package tours to Corfu are sold.

Well, it's been a good life, she concluded, with a little nod of thanks towards the late Mr Pargeter for making it so.

Then she had a thought.

Pagan, ridiculous, yes, but she wasn't in a position to take too long in assessing the pros and cons of any course of action.

She'd tried prayer. All that had brought her had been release from Sergeant Karaskakis and his replacement by Spiro. Out of the frying pan, all too literally into the fire.

But then maybe her prayers had been misaddressed. When in Rome and all that . . . Got to abide by local customs, after all, haven't you?

And it couldn't do any harm.

'St Spiridon!' Mrs Pargeter loudly supplicated. 'Please save our lives!'

41

Now of course the wind could have been about to change at that moment, anyway. Winds do change all the time for no particular reason – it's regarded as part and parcel of the job, if you happen to be born a wind – and they are particularly prone to variation near the sea shore.

But the speed with which those flames, at one moment about to swallow up the wooden hut, had in the next changed their minds and retreated, leaving only skeletal vestiges of smouldering brush in their wake, did seem more than coincidental.

Mrs Pargeter was not by nature superstitious, but thereafter she always felt a particular affection for the memory of St Spiridon and, in subsequent moments of extremity, was more than once heard to invoke his name.

The recession of the flames, which consumed lustily everything they found in their path to the point of the headland, coincided with the return to consciousness of Larry Lambeth. After a few minutes of reorientation, he released the two women from their bonds.

As they were easing their stiffened limbs, they heard approaching shouts and saw a crowd hurrying up from the village. Arming themselves with branches of brushwood, the men of Agios Nikitas attacked the fire's last pockets of resistance.

And soon they heard drawing near the drone of the first fire-fighting aeroplane.

By romantic serendipity, it was Yianni who first entered the hut to check if anything was alight in there. And a romantic novelist might have observed, from the enthusiasm with which she threw herself into his arms, that the only flame therein was the one that burned in Conchita's heart.

It was only when the last sparks of the real fire were being extinguished that the bodies were found.

Sergeant Karaskakis, fleeing from the flames, had stumbled over the cliff edge and broken his neck on the rocks below.

Spiro, by contrast, had stood his ground and the flames had consumed him so thoroughly that he could only be identified by a process of elimination.

St Spiridon had not only answered Mrs Pargeter's prayer, but had also, with a godlike facility for killing two birds with one stone, contrived at the same time to fulfil the prophecy of the older Spiro Karaskakis.

42

It was the last evening of the fortnight's package. Last visits had been paid to favourite beaches. The minimarket had been raided for souvenirs – sponges, ceramic drink mats, 'No Problem' T-shirts, lighters with outlines of Corfu on them, pencils topped by white-skirted soldiers, and a good few ouzo bottles in the shape of classical Greek columns. A few people had even bought retsina, under the mistaken impression that it would taste the same when they got it home.

And now everyone had homed in on their favourite taverna for that last celebratory meal. Before the end of the evening a good few would have pushed the boat out by ordering what the menu inaccurately called lobster 'because, after all, it's our last night', others would have made the unwise decision to give the old Greek brandy a bashing 'because, after all, it's our last night', while yet more would have made rash promises to taverna-owners and waiters that they 'really would be back next year'.

And the taverna-owners and waiters of Agios Nikitas would have nodded and smiled farewell with those assurances of undying friendship which they would accord impartially to every departing visitor of the summer, before they retired to Agralias to spend the winter moaning about the decline in the tourist trade.

Though she had been well looked after at the Hotel Nausica, it did not occur to Mrs Pargeter to spend her last evening anywhere other than Spiro's taverna. Or rather Yianni's taverna, as it now was.

The young man had come to the inheritance by an easier route than his predecessor, but already showed signs of a new maturity in handling its responsibilities. With the help of his aunt Theodosia, who was taking the first faltering steps back to normal life, he promised to be a good businessman.

Already he had demonstrated a steelier side of his nature by cutting off a long-standing credit account. If Georgio wanted to continue drinking ouzo all day, from now on he was going to have to pay for it.

Georgio, soon realising that he didn't actually have any money, had turned to Ginnie and been astonished to have his appeals turned down. The worm had finally turned and she walked out on him, announcing that at the end of the season she would return permanently to England. Georgio felt confident that he could probably woo her back, but somehow never got round to doing anything about it.

After a couple of days without the means to buy drink, he readily succumbed to Yianni's offer of a job in the kitchen, where he was destined to spend the rest of his life washing up and dreaming of ever more impracticable ways of making money.

That last evening Conchita had been sitting with Mrs Pargeter, but had just gone inside the taverna. That's where she'd spent most of the evenings of the last week, sitting at the bar with a drink under the benign gaze of old Spiro, and trying to get some attention from an increasingly preoccupied Yianni.

Mrs Pargeter looked around at the crowd under the awning.

Linda from South Woodham Ferrers was regretting her decision to see whether Craig liked moussaka, as she picked oily slivers of aubergine off the white tasselled 'Corfu Sport' T-shirt she'd bought that afternoon. Keith from South Woodham Ferrers was poring over the menu with his calculator, trying to estimate the bill for that evening's meal and come up with an overall total for what the holiday had cost them. He really wouldn't mind getting back to the office now. Been feeling that for most of the last week, actually. Great to get away, of course, but a fortnight was a long time.

At another table the Secretary with Short Bleached Hair and the Secretary with Long Bleached Hair, now both more or less uniformly brown, were sitting with two squaddies they'd picked up the night before in a disco in Dassia and invited for the evening. The boys had hitched a lift to Agios Nikitas, but there was no way they'd be able to get back that night. Which of course meant that they'd have to come back to the villa. Which meant they'd try and get into bed with the girls. Which wasn't a problem in itself. But for the fact that both girls fancied the tall Yorkshire one with the butterfly tattooed on his shoulder, and neither fancied the short Welsh one with the snake tattooed up his right leg. They watched each other warily, trying to cover every move.

At another table Mr Safari Suit was setting some

new arrivals at their ease. 'Been very hot today, hasn't it? Cor! Phew!'

The new arrivals decided it really was time they got their bill. Mr Safari Suit comforted himself by arranging Mrs Safari Suit artistically against the taverna wall for the 'and this was on our last evening' shot.

Mrs Pargeter decided it really hadn't been a bad fortnight. Not sure that she'd choose to go on a package holiday again, though.

She let out a little shudder as she contemplated the next day's arrangements – the steamy queueing at Corfu Airport, the inevitable delay in the departure lounge, the plastic food in the crowded plane. No, next time, she decided, she'd let Hamish Ramon Henriques make her holiday arrangements. His attitude to the business of travel was comfortingly close to that of the late Mr Pargeter.

She saw Conchita coming out of the taverna towards her, and felt a momentary pang for Joyce's death. Conchita would be travelling back tomorrow by scheduled flight, but her enjoyment of that comfort might be inhibited by the knowledge that her mother's coffin was accompanying her.

The suicide verdict, incidentally, had been ratified, which was fine by Mrs Pargeter. She didn't care whether official records were right or wrong, so long as she herself knew that justice had been done.

'Yianni busy?' she asked, as Conchita sat down.

'So what else is new?'

'Sorry you'll be saying goodbye to him tomorrow?'

'I'll survive.'

'Think you'll be back to see him again soon?'

Conchita laughed and shook her head. 'No way. Beautiful he may be, but he's as conventional as hell. Deeply shocked when I suggested he should go to bed with me.'

Mrs Pargeter, not for the first time, contemplated the

cultural differences between the Corfiots and the tourists who provided their pitta bread and butter. Must put quite a strain on the men, she imagined, being surrounded all day by half-naked tourists and then going back to the rigid peasant morality of their homes.

'No,' Conchita was saying, 'only way I could come back here to Yianni would be if I married him.' A shiver passed through her. 'Just imagine it. No, most of the men I know in London may be bastards, but at least they sometimes let me be myself.'

Suddenly Mrs Pargeter stopped feeling sorry for Conchita. The girl kept meeting bastards because she wanted to meet bastards and she'd go on doing it all her life. What was more, she'd see to it that she gave them at least as much hell as they gave her.

'Hello, Mrs P. Conchita.'

Larry Lambeth had bustled up to join them. He waved to a waiter for more drinks, sat down and handed a brown envelope across to Mrs Pargeter.

'Here it is.'

No one had been able to find her passport after Sergeant Karaskakis' death. She had said maybe she should get on to the British Consul to organise a replacement, but Larry Lambeth wouldn't hear of it. 'Take for ever, that would. You leave it with me. Fact is, I'd be insulted if you didn't,' he'd said, and winked.

She pulled out the passport and studied it. 'It looks terrific.'

He smiled with quiet pride. 'Quite pleased with it myself. A first for me, actually, you know.'

'Oh, really?'

'First time I've ever had to do one for someone's real identity.'

'Ah,' said Mrs Pargeter.

She was about to ask where he'd got the original

passport which he had so skilfully doctored, but stopped herself in time.

She recognised yet another of those situations when it wasn't necessary for her to know all the details. The late Mr Pargeter had trained her frightfully well.